Violets and Other Tales

VIOLETS
AND OTHER TALES

Alice Ruth Moore Dunbar Nelson

1895

AMIKA PRESS
NORTHFIELD IL 2022

First Edition   ISBN 13: 978-1-956872-90-3
AMIKA PRESS CLASSICS   466 Central Ave #23 Northfield IL 60093
847 920 8084   info@amikapress.com

Designed & typeset by Sarah Koz in 2022. Body & titles in Plantin, designed by Frank Hinman Pierpont in 1912–14, digitized by Monotype in 1990. Ornaments in ITC Bodoni Ornaments, designed by Giambattista Bodoni in 1790 and Janice Fishman, Holly Goldsmith, Jim Parkinson & Sumner Stone in 1995. Cover illustration by Ferro Rubini, Shutterstock.

Thanks to Courtney Kieras Porter, Marilee Rose Rutherford, John K Manos, Nathan Matteson & Jay Amberg.

To my friend of November 5th, 1892
—*A. R. M.*

INTRODUCTION.

In this day when the world is fairly teeming with books,—good books, books written with a motive, books inculcating morals, books teaching lessons,—it seems almost a piece of presumption too great for endurance to foist another upon the market. There is scarcely room in the literary world for amateurs and maiden efforts; the very worthiest are sometimes poorly repaid for their best efforts. Yet, another one is offered the public, a maiden effort,—a little thing with absolutely nothing to commend it, that seeks to do nothing more than amuse.

Many of these sketches and verses have appeared in print before, in newspapers and a magazine or two; many are seeing the light of day for the first time. If perchance this collection of idle thoughts may serve to while away an hour or two, or lift for a brief space the load of care from someone's mind, their purpose has been served —the author is satisfied.

A. R. M.

CONTENTS.

1—VIOLETS.

4—THREE THOUGHTS.

6—THE WOMAN.

10—TEN MINUTES' MUSING.

13—A PLAINT.

14—IN UNCONSCIOUSNESS.

18—TITEE.

24—ANARCHY ALLEY.

28—IMPRESSIONS.

30—SALAMMBÔ BY GUSTAVE FLAUBERT.

33—LEGEND OF THE NEWSPAPER.

36—A CARNIVAL JANGLE.

40—PAUL TO VIRGINIA. FIN DE SIECLE.

42—THE MAIDEN'S DREAM.

46—IN MEMORIAM.

49—A STORY OF VENGEANCE.

53—AT BAY ST. LOUIS.

54—NEW YEAR'S DAY.

55—THE UNKNOWN LIFE OF JESUS CHRIST.

61—IN OUR NEIGHBORHOOD.

68—FAREWELL.

70—LITTLE MISS SOPHIE.

77—IF I HAD KNOWN.

78—CHALMETLE.

81—AT EVENTIDE.

85—THE IDLER.

86—LOVE AND THE BUTTERFLY.

87—THE BEE-MAN.

90—AMID THE ROSES.

PREFACE.

These fugitive pieces are launched upon the tide of public opinion to sink or swim upon their merit. They will float for a while, but whether they will reach the haven of popularity depends upon their enduring qualities. Some will surely perish, many will reach some port, but time alone will tell if any shall successfully breast the ocean of thought and plant its standard upon the summit of fame.

When one enters the domain of authorship, she places herself at the mercy of critics. Were she as sure of being commended by the best and most intelligent of her readers, as she is sure of being condemned by the worst and most ignorant, there would still be a thrill of pleasure in all criticism, for the satisfaction of having received the praise of the first would compensate for the harshness of the latter. Just criticism is wholesome and never wounds the sensibilities of the true author, for it saves her from the danger of an excess of pride which is the greatest foe to individual progress, while it spurs her on to loftier flights and nobler deeds. A poor writer is bad, but a poor critic is worse, therefore, unjust criticism should never ruffle the temper of its victim. The author of these pages belongs to that type of the "brave new woman who scorns to sigh," but feels that she has something to say, and says it to the best of her ability, and leaves the verdict in the hands of the public. She gives to the reader her best thoughts and leaves him to accept or reject as merit may manifest itself. No author is under contract to please her readers at all times, nor can she hope to control the sentiments of all of them at any time, therefore, the obligation is reciprocal, for the fame she receives is due to the pleasure she affords.

The author of these fugitive pieces is young, just on the threshold of life, and with the daring audacity of youth makes assertions and gives decisions which she may reverse as time mellows her opinions, and the realities of life force aside the theories of youth, and prosy facts obscure the memory of that happy time when the heart overflowing with——

> "The joy
> Of young ideas painted on the mind,
> In the warm glowing colors Fancy spreads
> On objects, not yet known, when all is new,
> And all is lovely."

There is much in this book that is good; much that is crude; some that is poor: but all give that assurance of something great and noble when the bud of promise, now unfolding its petals in the morning glow of light, will have matured into that fuller growth of blossoming flower ere the noonday sun passes its zenith. May the hope thus engendered by this first attempt reach its fruition, and may the energy displayed by one so young meet the reward it merits from an approving public.

Sylvanie F. Williams.

VIOLETS.

I.

"And she tied a bunch of violets with a tress of her pretty brown hair."

She sat in the yellow glow of the lamplight softly humming these words. It was Easter evening, and the newly risen spring world was slowly sinking to a gentle, rosy, opalescent slumber, sweetly tired of the joy which had pervaded it all day. For in the dawn of the perfect morn, it had arisen, stretched out its arms in glorious happiness to greet the Saviour and said its hallelujahs, merrily trilling out carols of bird, and organ and flower-song. But the evening had come, and rest.

There was a letter lying on the table, it read:

"Dear, I send you this little bunch of flowers as my Easter token. Perhaps you may not be able to read their meaning, so I'll tell you. Violets, you know, are my favorite flowers. Dear, little, human-faced things! They seem always as if about to whisper a love-word; and then they signify that thought which passes always between you and me. The orange blossoms—you know their meaning; the little pinks are the flowers you love; the evergreen leaf is the symbol of the endurance of our affection; the tube-roses I put in, because once when you kissed and pressed me close in your arms, I had a bunch of tube-roses on my bosom, and the heavy fragrance of their crushed loveliness has always lived in my memory. The violets and pinks are from a bunch I wore to-day, and when kneeling at the altar, during communion, did I sin, dear, when I thought of you? The tube-roses and orange-blossoms I wore Friday night; you always wished for a lock of my hair, so I'll tie these flowers with them—but there, it is not stable enough; let me wrap them with a bit of ribbon, pale blue, from that little dress I wore last winter to the dance, when we had such a long, sweet talk in that forgotten nook. You always loved that dress, it fell in such soft ruffles away from the throat and bosom,—you called me your little forget-me-not, that night. I laid the flowers away for awhile in our favorite book,—Byron—just at the poem we loved best, and now I send them to you. Keep them always in remembrance of me, and if aught should occur to separate us, press these flowers to your lips, and I will be with you in spirit, permeating your heart with unutterable love and happiness."

II.

It is Easter again. As of old, the joyous bells clang out the glad news of the resurrection. The giddy, dancing sunbeams laugh riotously in field and street; birds carol their sweet twitterings everywhere, and the heavy perfume of flowers scents the golden atmosphere with inspiring fragrance. One long, golden sunbeam steals silently into the white-curtained window of a quiet room, and lay athwart a sleeping face. Cold, pale, still, its fair, young face pressed against the satin-lined casket. Slender, white fingers, idle now, they that had never known rest; locked softly over a bunch of violets; violets and tube-roses in her soft, brown hair, violets in the bosom of her long, white gown; violets and tube-roses and orange-blossoms banked everywhere, until the air was filled with the ascending souls of the human flowers. Some whispered that a broken heart had ceased to flutter in that still, young form, and that it was a mercy for the soul to ascend on the slender sunbeam. To-day she kneels at the throne of heaven, where one year ago she had communed at an earthly altar.

III.

Far away in a distant city, a man, carelessly looking among some papers, turned over a faded bunch of flowers tied with a blue ribbon and a lock of hair. He paused meditatively awhile, then turning to the regal-looking woman lounging before the fire, he asked:

"Wife, did you ever send me these?"

She raised her great, black eyes to his with a gesture of ineffable disdain, and replied languidly:

"You know very well I can't bear flowers. How could I ever send such sentimental trash to any one? Throw them into the fire."

And the Easter bells chimed a solemn requiem as the flames slowly licked up the faded violets. Was it merely fancy on the wife's part, or did the husband really sigh,—a long, quivering breath of remembrance?

THREE THOUGHTS.

FIRST

How few of us
In all the world's great, ceaseless struggling strife,
Go to our work with gladsome, buoyant step,
And love it for its sake, whate'er it be.
Because it is a labor, or, mayhap,
Some sweet, peculiar art of God's own gift;
And not the promise of the world's slow smile
of recognition, or of mammon's gilded grasp.
Alas, how few, in inspiration's dazzling flash,
Or spiritual sense of world's beyond the dome
Of circling blue around this weary earth,
Can bask, and know the God-given grace
Of genius' fire that flows and permeates
The virgin mind alone; the soul in which
The love of earth hath tainted not.
The love of art and art alone.

SECOND

"Who dares stand forth?" the monarch cried,
  "Amid the throng, and dare to give
    Their aid, and bid this wretch to live?
I pledge my faith and crown beside,
A woeful plight, a sorry sight,
  This outcast from all God-given grace.

What, ho! in all, no friendly face,
No helping hand to stay his plight?
St. Peter's name be pledged for aye,
   The man's accursed, that is true;
   But ho, he suffers. None of you
Will mercy show, or pity sigh?"

Strong men drew back, and lordly train
   Did slowly file from monarch's look,
   Whose lips curled scorn. But from a nook
A voice cried out, "Though he has slain
That which I loved the best on earth,
   Yet will I tend him till he dies,
   I can be brave." A woman's eyes
Gazed fearlessly into his own.

THIRD

When all the world has grown full cold to thee,
And man—proud pygmy—shrugs all scornfully,
And bitter, blinding tears flow gushing forth,
Because of thine own sorrows and poor plight,
Then turn ye swift to nature's page,
And read there passions, immeasurably far
Greater than thine own in all their littleness.
For nature has her sorrows and her joys,
As all the piled-up mountains and low vales
Will silently attest—and hang thy head
In dire confusion, for having dared
To moan at thine own miseries
When God and nature suffer silently.

THE WOMAN.

The literary manager of the club arose, cleared his throat, adjusted his cravat, fixed his eyes sternly upon the young man, and in a sonorous voice, a little marred by his habitual lisp, asked: "Mr. ——, will you please tell us your opinion upon the question, whether woman's chances for matrimony are increased or decreased when she becomes man's equal as a wage earner?"

The secretary adjusted her eye-glass, and held her pencil alertly poised above her book, ready to note which side Mr. —— took. Mr. —— fidgeted, pulled himself together with a violent jerk, and finally spoke his mind. Someone else did likewise, also someone else, then the women interposed, and jumped on the men, the men retaliated, a wordy war ensued, and the whole matter ended by nothing being decided, pro or con—generally the case in wordy discussions. *Moi?* Well, I sawed wood and said nothing, but all the while there was forming in my mind, no, I won't say forming, it was there already. It was this, *Why should well-salaried women marry?* Take the average working-woman of to-day. She works from five to ten hours a day, doing extra night work, sometimes, of course. Her work over, she goes home or to her boarding-house, as the case may be. Her meals are prepared for her, she has no household cares upon her shoulders, no troublesome dinners to prepare for a fault-finding husband, no fretful children to try her patience, no petty bread and meat economies to adjust. She has her cares, her money-troubles, her debts, and her scrimpings, it is true, but they only make her independent, instead of reducing her to a dead level of despair. Her day's work ends at the office, school, factory or store; the rest of the time is hers, undisturbed by the restless going to and fro of housewifely cares, and she can employ it in mental or social diversions. She does not incessantly rely upon the whims of a cross man to take her to such amusements as she desires. In this nineteenth century she is free to go where she pleases—provided it be in a moral atmosphere—without comment. Theatres, concerts, lectures, and the lighter amusements of social affairs among her associates, are open to her, and there she can go, see, and be seen, admire and be admired, enjoy and be enjoyed, without a single harrowing thought of the baby's milk or the husband's coffee.

Her earnings are her own, indisputably, unreservedly, undividedly. She knows to a certainty just how much she can spend, how well she can dress, how far her earnings will go. If there is a dress, a book, a bit of music, a bunch of flowers, or a bit of furniture that she wants, she can get it, and there is no need of asking anyone's advice, or gently hinting to John that Mrs. So and So has a lovely new hat, and there is one ever so much prettier and cheaper down at Thus & Co.'s. To an independent spirit there is a certain sense of humiliation and wounded pride in asking for money, be it five cents or five hundred dollars. The working woman knows no such pang; she has but to question her account and all is over. In the summer she takes her savings of the winter, packs her trunk and takes a trip more or less extensive, and there is none to say her nay,—nothing to bother her save the accumulation of her own baggage. There is an independent, happy, free-and-easy swing about the motion of her life. Her mind is constantly being broadened by contact with the world in its working clothes; in her leisure moments by the better thoughts of dead and living men which she meets in her applications to books and periodicals; in her vacations, by her studies of nature, or it may be other communities than her own. The freedom which she enjoys she does not trespass upon, for if she did not learn at school she has acquired since habits of strong self-reliance, self-support, earnest thinking, deep discriminations, and firmly believes that the most perfect liberty is that state in which humanity conforms itself to and obeys strictly, without deviation, those laws which are best fitted for their mutual self-advancement.

And so your independent working woman of to day comes as near being ideal in her equable self poise as can be imagined. So why should she hasten to give this liberty up in exchange for a serfdom, sweet sometimes, it is true, but which too often becomes galling and unendurable.

It is not marriage that I decry, for I don't think any really sane person would do this, but it is this wholesale marrying of girls in their teens, this rushing into an unknown plane of life to avoid work. Avoid work! What housewife dares call a moment her own?

Marriages might be made in Heaven, but too often they are consummated right here on earth, based on a desire to possess the physical attractions of the woman by the man, pretty much as a child desires a toy, and an innate love of man, a wild desire not to be ridiculed by the foolish as an "old maid," and a certain delicate shrinking from the work of the world—laziness is a good name for it—by the woman. The attraction of mind to mind, the ability of one to compliment the lights and shadows in the other, the capacity of either to fulfil the duties of wife or husband—these do not enter into the contract. That is why we have divorce courts.

And so our independent woman in every year of her full, rich, well-rounded life, gaining fresh knowledge and experience, learning humanity, and particularly that portion of it which is the other gender, so well as to avoid clay-footed idols, and finally when she does consent to bear the yoke upon her shoulders, does so with perhaps less romance and glamor than her younger scoffing sisters, but with an assurance of solid and more lasting happiness. Why should she have hastened this; was aught lost by the delay?

"They say" that men don't admire this type of woman, that they prefer the soft, dainty, winning, mindless creature who cuddles into men's arms, agrees to everything they say, and looks upon them as a race of gods turned loose upon this earth for the edification of womankind. Well, may be so, but there is one thing positive, they certainly respect the independent one, and admire her, too, even if it is at a distance, and that in itself is something. As to the other part, no matter how sensible a woman is on other questions, when she falls in love she is fool enough to believe her adored one a veritable Solomon. Cuddling? Well, she may preside over conventions, brandish her umbrella at board meetings, tramp the streets soliciting subscriptions, wield the blue pencil in an editorial sanctum, hammer a type-writer, smear her nose with ink from a galley full of pied type, lead infant ideas through the tortuous mazes of c-a-t and r-a-t, plead at the bar, or wield the scalpel in a dissecting room, yet when the right moment comes, she will sink as gracefully into his manly embrace, throw her arms as lovingly around his neck, and cuddle as warmly and sweetly to his bosom as her little sister who has done nothing else but think, dream, and practice for that hour. It comes natural, you see.

TEN MINUTES' MUSING.

There was a terrible noise in the school-yard at intermission; peeping out the windows the boys could be seen huddled in an immense bunch, in the middle of the yard. It looked like a fight, a mob, a knock-down,—anything, so we rushed out to the door hastily, fearfully, ready to scold, punish, console, frown, bind up broken heads or drag wounded forms from the melee as the case might be. Nearly every boy in the school was in that seething, swarming mass, and those who weren't were standing around on the edges, screaming and throwing up their hats in hilarious excitement. It was a mob, a fearful mob, but a mob apparently with a vigorous and well-defined purpose. It was a mob that screamed and howled, and kicked, and yelled, and shouted, and perspired, and squirmed, and wriggled, and pushed, and threatened, and poured itself all seemingly upon some central object. It was a mob that had an aim, that was determined to accomplish that aim, even though the whole azure expanse of sky fell upon them. It was a mob with set muscles, straining like whipcords, eyes on that central object and with heads inward and sturdy legs outward, like prairie horses reversed in a battle. The cheerers and hat throwers on the outside were mirthful, but the mob was not; it howled, but howled without any cachinnation; it struggled for mastery. Some fell and were trampled over, some weaker ones were even tossed in the air, but the mob never deigned to trouble itself about such trivialities. It was an interesting, nervous whole, with divers parts of separate vitality.

In alarm I looked about for the principal. He was standing at a safe distance with his hands in his pockets watching the seething mass with a broad smile. At sight of my perplexed expression some one was about to venture an explanation, when there was a wild yell, a sudden vehement disintegration of the mass, a mighty rush and clutch at a dark object bobbing in the air—and the mist cleared from my intellect—as I realized it all—football.

Did you ever stop to see the analogy between a game of football and the interesting little game called life which we play every day? There is one, far-fetched as it may seem, though, for that matter, life's game, being one of desperate chances and strategic moves, is analogous to anything.

But, if we could get out of ourselves and soar above the world, far enough to view the mass beneath in its daily struggles, and near enough the hearts of the people to feel the throbs beneath their boldly carried exteriors, the whole would seem naught but such a maddening rush and senseless-looking crushing. "We are but children of a larger growth" after all, and our ceaseless pursuing after the baubles of this earth are but the struggles for precedence in the business play-ground.

The football is money. See how the mass rushes after it! Everyone so intent upon his pursuit until all else dwindles into a ridiculous nonentity. The weaker ones go down in the mad pursuit, and are unmercifully trampled upon, but no matter, what is the difference if the foremost win the coveted prize and carry it off. See the big boy in front, he with iron grip, and determined, compressed lips? That boy is a type of the big, merciless man, the Gradgrind of the latter century. His face is set towards the ball, and even though he may crush a dozen small boys, he'll make his way through the mob and come out triumphant. And he'll be the victor longer than anyone else, in spite of the envy and fighting and pushing about him.

To an observer, alike unintelligent about the rules of a football game, and the conditions which govern the barter and exchange and fluctuations of the world's money market, there is as much difference between the sight of a mass of boys on a play-ground losing their equilibrium over a spheroid of rubber and a mass of men losing their coolness and temper and mental and nervous balance on change as there is between a pine sapling and a mighty forest king—merely a difference of age. The mighty, seething, intensely concentrated mass in its emphatic tendency to one point is the same, in the utter disregard of mental and physical welfare. The momentary triumphs of transitory possessions impress a casual looker-on with the same fearful idea—that the human race, after all, is savage to the core, and cultivates its savagery in an inflated happiness at own nearness to perfection.

But the bell clangs sharply, the overheated, nervous, tingling boys fall into line, and the sudden transition from massing disorder to military precision cuts short the ten minutes' musing.

A PLAINT.

Dear God, 'tis hard, so awful hard to lose
The one we love, and see him go afar,
With scarce one thought of aching hearts behind,
Nor wistful eyes, nor outstretched yearning hands.
Chide not, dear God, if surging thoughts arise.
And bitter questionings of love and fate,
But rather give my weary heart thy rest,
And turn the sad, dark memories into sweet.
Dear God, I fain my loved one were anear,
But since thou will'st that happy thence he'll be,
I send him forth, and back I'll choke the grief
Rebellious rises in my lonely heart.
I pray thee, God, my loved one joy to bring;
I dare not hope that joy will be with me,
But ah, dear God, one boon I crave of thee,
That he shall ne'er forget his hours with me.

IN UNCONSCIOUSNESS.

There was a big booming in my ears, great heavy iron bells that swung to-and-fro on either side, and sent out deafening reverberations that steeped the senses in a musical melody of sonorous sound; to-and-fro, backward and forward, yet ever receding in a gradually widening circle, monotonous, mournful, weird, suffusing the soul with an unutterable sadness, as images of wailing processions, of weeping, empty-armed women, and widowed maidens flashed through the mind, and settled on the soul with a crushing, o'er-pressing weight of sorrow.

Now I lay floating, arms outstretched, on an illimitable waste of calm tranquil waters. Far away as eye could reach, there was naught but the pale, white-flecked, green waters of this ocean of eternity, and above the tender blue sky arched down in perfect love of its mistress, the ocean. Sky and sea, sea and sky, blue, calm, infinite, perfect sea, heaving its womanly bosom to the passionate kisses of its ardent sun-lover. Away into infinity stretched this perfectibility of love; into eternity, I was drifting, alone, silent, yet burdened still with the remembrance of the sadness of the bells.

Far away, they tolled out the incessant dirge, grown resignedly sweet now; so intense in its infinite peace, that a calm of love, beyond all human understanding and above all earthly passions, sank deep into my soul, and so permeated my whole being with rest and peace, that my lips smiled and my eyes drooped in access of fulsome joy. Into the illimitable space of infinity we drifted, my soul and I, borne along only by the network of auburn hair that floated about me in the green waters.

But now, a rude grasp from somewhere is laid upon me, pressing upon my face. Instantly the air grows gloomy, gray, and the ocean rocks menacingly, while the great bells grow harsh and strident, as they hint of a dark fate. I clasp my hands appealingly to the heavens; I moan and struggle with the unknown grasp; then there is peace and the sweet content of the infinite Nirvana.

Then slowly, softly, the net of auburn hair begins to drag me down below the surface of the sea. Oh! the skies are so sweet, and now that the tender stars are looking upon us, how fair to stay and sway upon the breast of eternity! But the net is inexorable, and gently, slowly pulls me down. Now we sink straight, now we whirl in slow, eddying circles, spiral-like; while at each turn those bells ring out clanging now in wild crescendo, then whispering dread secrets of the ocean's depths. Oh, ye mighty bells, tell me from your learned lore of the hopes of mankind! Tell me what fruit he beareth from his strivings and yearnings; know not ye? Why ring ye now so joyful, so hopeful; then toll your dismal prophecies of o'er-cast skies?

Years have passed, and now centuries, too, are swallowed in the gulf of eternity, yet the auburn net still whirls me in eddying circles, down, down to the very womb of time; to the innermost recesses of the mighty ocean.

And now, peace, perfect, unconditioned, sublime peace, and rest, and silence. For to the great depths of the mighty ocean the solemn bells cannot penetrate, and no sound, not even the beatings of one's own heart, is heard. In the heart of eternity there can be nothing to break the calm of frozen æons. In the great white hall I lay, silent, unexpectant, calm, and smiled in perfect content at the web of auburn hair which trailed across my couch. No passionate longing for life or love, no doubting question of heaven or hell, no strife for carnal needs,—only rest, content, peace—happiness, perfect, whole, complete, sublime.

And thus passed ages and ages, æons and æons. The great earth there in the dim distance above the ocean has toiled wearily about the sun, until its mechanism was failing, and the warm ardor of the lover's eye was becoming pale and cold from age, while the air all about the fast dwindling sphere was heavy and thick with the sorrows and heartaches and woes of the humans upon its face. Heavy with the screams and roar of war; with the curses of the deceived of traitors; with the passionate sighs of unlawful love; with the crushing unrest of blighted hopes. Knowledge and contempt of all these things permeated even to the inmost depths of time, as I lay in the halls of rest and smiled at the web floating through my white fingers.

But hark! discord begins. There is a vague fear which springs from an unknown source and drifts into the depths of rest; fear, indefinable, unaccountable, unknowable, shuddering. Pain begins, for the heart springs into life, and fills the silence with the terror of its beatings, thick, knifing, frightful in its intense longing. Power of mind over soul, power of calm over fear avail nothing; suspense and misery, locked arm in arm, pervade æonic stillness, till all things else become subordinate, unnoticed.

Centuries drift away, and the giddy, old reprobate—earth, dying a hideous, ghastly death, with but one solitary human to shudder in unison with its last throes, to bask in the last pale rays of a cold sun, to inhale the last breath of a metallic atmosphere; totters, reels, falls into space, and is no more. Peal out, ye brazen bells, peal out the requiem of the sinner! Roll your mournful tones into the ears of the saddened angels, weeping with wing-covered eyes! Toll the requiem of the sinner, sinking swiftly, sobbingly into the depths of time's ocean. Down, down, until the great groans which arose from the domes and Ionic roofs about me told that the sad old earth sought rest in eternity, while the universe shrugged its shoulders over the loss of another star.

And now, the great invisible fear became apparent, tangible, for all the sins, the woes, the miseries, the dreads, the dismal achings and throbbings, the dreariness and gloom of the lost star came together and like a huge geni took form and hideous shape—octopus-like—which slowly approached me, erstwhile happy—and hovered about my couch in fearful menace.

Oh, shining web of hair, burst loose your bonds and bid me move! Oh, time, cease not your calculations, but speed me on to deliverance! Oh, silence, vast, immense, infuse into your soul some sound other than the heavy throbbing of this fast disintegrating heart! Oh, pitiless stone arches, let fall your crushing weight upon this Stygian monster!

I pray to time, to eternity, to the frozen æons of the past. Useless. I am seized, forced to open my cold lips; there is agony,—supreme, mortal agony of nerve tension, and wrenching of vitality. I struggle, scream, and clutching the monster with superhuman strength, fling him aside, and rise, bleeding, screaming—but triumphant, and keenly mortal in every vein, alive and throbbing with consciousness and pain.

No, it was not opium, nor night-mare, but chloroform, a dentist, three obstinate molars, a pair of forceps, and a lively set of nerves.

TITEE.

It was cold that day; the great sharp north wind swept out Elysian-fields Street in blasts that made men shiver, and bent everything in its track. The skies hung lowering and gloomy; the usually quiet street was more than deserted, it was dismal.

Titee leaned against one of the brown freight cars for protection against the shrill norther, and warmed his little chapped hands at a blaze of chips and dry grass. "May be it'll snow," he muttered, casting a glance at the sky that would have done credit to a practised seaman. "Then *won't* I have fun! Ugh, but the wind blows!"

It was Saturday, or Titee would have been in school—the big yellow school on Marigny Street, where he went every day when its bell boomed nine o'clock. Went with a run and a joyous whoop,—presumably to imbibe knowledge, ostensibly to make his teacher's life a burden.

Idle, lazy, dirty, troublesome boy, she called him, to herself, as day by day wore on, and Titee improved not, but let his whole class pass him on its way to a higher grade. A practical joke he relished infinitely more than a practical problem, and a good game at pin-sticking was far more entertaining than a language lesson. Moreover, he was always hungry, and *would* eat in school before the half-past ten intermission, thereby losing much good play-time for his voracious appetite.

But there was nothing in natural history that Titee didn't know. He could dissect a butterfly or a mosquito-hawk and describe their parts as accurately as a spectacled student with a scalpel and microscope could talk about a cadaver. The entire Third District, with its swamps and canals and commons and railroad sections, and its wondrous, crooked, tortuous streets was as an open book to Titee.

There was not a nook or corner that he did not know or could tell of. There was not a bit of gossip among the gamins, little Creole and Spanish fellows, with dark skins and lovely eyes like Spaniels, that Titee could not tell of. He knew just exactly when it was time for crawfish to be plentiful down in the Claiborne and Marigny canals; just when a poor, breadless fellow might get a job in the big bone-yard and fertilizing factory out on the railroad track; and as for the levee, with its ships and schooners and sailors—Oh, how he could revel among them! The wondrous ships, the pretty little schooners, where the foreign-looking sailors lay on long moon-lit nights, singing gay bar carols to the tinkle of a guitar and mandolin. All these things, and more, could Titee tell of. He had been down to the Gulf, and out on its treacherous waters through Eads Jetties on a fishing smack, with some jolly, brown sailors, and could interest the whole school-room in the "talk lessons," if he chose.

Titee shivered as the wind swept round the freight cars. There isn't much warmth in a bit of a jersey coat.

"Wish 'twas summer," he murmured, casting another sailor's glance at the sky. "Don't believe I like snow, it's too wet and cold." And, with a last parting caress at the little fire he had built for a minute's warmth, he plunged his hands in his pockets, shut his teeth, and started manfully on his mission out the railroad track towards the swamps.

It was late when Titee came home, to such a home as it was, and he had but illy performed his errand, so his mother beat him, and sent him to bed supperless. A sharp strap stings in cold weather, and long walks in the teeth of a biting wind creates a keen appetite. But if Titee cried himself to sleep that night, he was up bright and early next morning, and had been to early mass, devoutly kneeling on the cold floor, blowing his fingers to keep them warm, and was home almost before the rest of the family was awake.

There was evidently some great matter of business in this young man's mind, for he scarcely ate his breakfast, and had left the table, eagerly cramming the remainder of his meal in his pockets.

"I wonder what he's up to now?" mused his mother as she watched his little form sturdily trudging the track in the face of the wind, his head, with the rimless cap thrust close on the shock of black hair, bent low, his hands thrust deep in the bulging pockets.

"A new snake, perhaps," ventured the father; "he's a queer child."

But the next day Titee was late for school. It was something unusual, for he was always the first on hand to fix some plan of mechanism to make the teacher miserable. She looked reprovingly at him this morning, when he came in during the arithmetic class, his hair all wind-blown, cheeks rosy from a hard fight with the sharp blasts. But he made up for his tardiness by his extreme goodness all day; just think, Titee didn't even eat in school. A something unparalleled in the entire history of his school-life.

When the lunch-hour came, and all the yard was a scene of feast and fun, one of the boys found him standing by one of the posts, disconsolately watching a ham sandwich as it rapidly disappeared down the throat of a sturdy, square-headed little fellow.

"Hello, Edgar," he said, "What yer got fer lunch?"

"Nothin'," was the mournful reply.

"Ah, why don't yer stop eatin' in school fer a change? Yer don't ever have nothin' to eat."

"I didn't eat to-day," said Titee, blazing up.

"Yer did!"

"I tell you I didn't!" and Titee's hard little fist planted a punctuation mark on his comrade's eye.

A fight in the school-yard! Poor Titee in disgrace again. But in spite of his battered appearance, a severe scolding from the principal, lines to write, and a further punishment from his mother, Titee scarcely remained for his dinner, but was off, down the railroad track, with his pockets partly stuffed with the remnants of his scanty meal.

And the next day Titee was tardy again, and lunchless, too, and the next, and the next, until the teacher in despair sent a nicely printed note to his mother about him, which might have done some good, had not Titee taken great pains to tear it up on his way home.

But one day it rained, whole bucketfuls of water, that poured in torrents from a miserable angry sky. Too wet a day for bits of boys to be trudging to school, so Titee's mother thought, so kept him home to watch the weather through the window, fretting and fuming, like a regular storm-cloud in miniature. As the day wore on, and the storm did not abate, his mother had to keep a strong watch upon him, or he would have slipped away.

At last dinner came and went, and the gray soddenness of the skies deepened into the blackness of coming night. Someone called Titee to go to bed—and Titee was nowhere to be found.

Under the beds, in corners and closets, through the yard, and in such impossible places as the soap-dish and the water-pitcher even; but he had gone as completely as if he had been spirited away. It was of no use to call up the neighbors; he had never been near their houses, they affirmed, so there was nothing to do but to go to the railroad track, where little Titee had been seen so often trudging in the shrill north wind.

So with lantern and sticks, and his little yellow dog, the rescuing party started out the track. The rain had ceased falling, but the wind blew a tremendous gale, scurrying great, gray clouds over a fierce sky. It was not exactly dark, though in this part of the city, there was neither gas nor electricity, and surely on such a night as this, neither moon nor stars dared show their faces in such a grayness of sky; but a sort of all-diffused luminosity was in the air, as though the sea of atmosphere was charged with an ethereal phosphorescence.

Search as they would, there were no signs of poor little Titee. The soft earth between the railroad ties crumbled beneath their feet without showing any small tracks or foot-prints.

"Let us return," said the big brother, "he can't be here anyway."

"No, no," urged the mother, "I feel that he is; let's go on."

So on they went, slipping on the wet earth, stumbling over the loose rocks, until a sudden wild yelp from Tiger brought them to a standstill. He had rushed ahead of them, and his voice could be heard in the distance, howling piteously.

With a fresh impetus the little muddy party hurried forward. Tiger's yelps could be heard plainer and plainer, mingled now with a muffled wail, as of some one in pain.

And then, after awhile they found a pitiful little heap of wet and sodden rags, lying at the foot of a mound of earth and stones thrown upon the side of the track. It was little Titee with a broken leg, all wet and miserable, and moaning.

They picked him up tenderly, and started to carry him home. But he cried and clung to his mother, and begged not to go.

"He's got fever," wailed his mother.

"No, no, it's my old man. He's hungry," sobbed Titee, holding out a little package. It was the remnants of his dinner, wet and rain washed.

"What old man?" asked the big brother.

"My old man, oh, please, please don't go home until I see him, I'm not hurting much, I can go."

So yielding to his whim, they carried him further away, down the sides of the track up to an embankment or levee by the sides of the Marigny canal. Then Titee's brother, suddenly stopping, exclaimed:

"Why, here's a cave, a regular Robinson Cruso affair."

"It's my old man's cave," cried Titee; "oh, please go in, maybe he's dead."

There can't be much ceremony in entering a cave, there is but one thing to do, walk in. This they did, and holding high the lantern, beheld a strange sight. On a bed of straw and paper in one corner lay a withered, wizened, white-bearded old man, with wide eyes staring at the unaccustomed sight. In the corner lay a cow.

"It's my old man!" cried Titee, joyfully. "Oh, please, grandpa, I couldn't get here to-day, it rained all morning, and when I ran away this evening, I slipped down and broke something, and oh, grandpa, I'm so tired and hurty, and I'm so afraid you're hungry."

So the secret of Titee's jaunts out the railroad was out. In one of his trips around the swamp-land, he had discovered the old man dying from cold and hunger in the fields. Together they had found this cave, and Titee had gathered the straw and brush that scattered itself over the ground and made the bed. A poor old cow turned adrift by an ungrateful master, had crept in and shared the damp dwelling. And thither Titee had trudged twice a day, carrying his luncheon in the morning, and his dinner in the evening, the sole support of a half-dead cripple.

"There's a crown in Heaven for that child," said the officer to whom the case was referred.

And so there was, for we scattered winter roses on his little grave down in old St. Rocque's cemetery. The cold and rain, and the broken leg had told their tale.

ANARCHY ALLEY.

To the casual observer, the quaint, narrow, little alley that lies in the heart of the city is no more than any other of the numerous divisions of streets in which New Orleans delights. But to the idle wanderer, or he whose mission down its four squares of much trodden stones, is an aimless one,—whose eyes unforced to bend to the ground in thought of sordid ways and means, can peer at will into its quaint corners. Exchange Alley presents all the phases of a Latinized portion of America, a bit of Europe, perhaps, the restless, chafing, anarchistic Europe of to-day, in the midst of the quieter democratic institution of our republic.

It is Bohemia, pure and simple, Bohemia, in all its stages, from the beer saloon and the cheap book-store, to the cheaper cook shop and uncertain lodging house. There the great American institution, the wondrous monarch whom the country supports—the tramp—basks in superior comfort and contented, unmolested indolence. Idleness and labor, poverty and opulence, the honest, law-abiding workingman, and the reckless, restless anarchist, jostle side by side, and brush each other's elbows in terms of equality as they do nowhere else.

On the busiest thoroughfares in the city, just in the busiest part, between two of the most crowded and conservative of cross-streets, lies this alley of Latinism. One might almost pass it hurriedly, avoiding the crowds that cluster at this section of the streets, but upon turning into a narrow section, stone-paved, the place is entered, appearing to end one square distant, seeming to bar itself from the larger buildings by an aimless sort of iron affair, part railing, part posts. There is a conservative book-store at the entrance on one side, and an even more harmless clothing store on the other; then comes a saloon with many blind doors, behind which are vistas of tables, crowded and crowded with men drinking beer out of "globes," large, round, moony, common affairs. There is a dingy, pension-claim office, with cripples and sorrowful-looking women in black, sitting about on rickety chairs. Somehow, there is always an impression with me that the mourning dress and mournful looks are put on to impress the dispenser and adjuster. It is wicked, but what can one do if impressions come?

There are more little cuddies of places, dye-shops, tailors, and nondescript corners that seem to have no possible mission on earth and are sadly conscious of their aimlessness. Then the railing is reached, and the alley instead of ending has merely given itself an angular twist to the right, and extends three squares further, to a great, pale green dome, and stately entrance.

The calmly-thinking, quietly-laboring, cool and conservative world is for the nonce left behind. With the first stepping across Customhouse street, the place widens architecturally, and the atmosphere, too, seems impregnated with a sort of mental freedom, conducive to dangerous theorizing and broody reflections on the inequality of the classes. The sun shines in a strip in the centre, yellow and elusive, like gold; someone is rattling a gay galop on a piano somewhere; there is a sound of mens' voices in a heated discussion, a long whiff of pipe-smoke trails through the sunlight from the bar-room; the clink of glasses, the chink of silver, and the high treble of a woman's voice scolding a refractory child, mingle in incongruous melody.

Two-story houses all along; the first floor divided into cuddies, here a paper store, displaying ten-cent novels of detective stories with impossible cuts, illustrating impossible situations of the plot; dye-shops, jewelers, tailors, tin-smiths, cook-shops, intelligence offices—many of these, and some newspaper offices. On the second floor, balconies, dingy, iron-railed, with sickly box-plants, and decrepit garments airing and being turned and tended by disheveled, slip-shod women. Lodging-houses these, some of them, but one is forced to wonder why do the tenants sun their clothes so often? The lines stretched from posts to posts seem always filled with airing garments. Is it economy? And do the owners of the faded vests and patched coats hide in dusky corners while their only garments are receiving the benefit of Old Sol's cleansing rays? And are the women with the indiscriminate tresses, near relatives, or only the landladies? It would be something worth knowing if one could.

Plenty of saloons—great, gorgeous, gaudy places, with pianos and swift-footed waiters, tables and cards, and men, men, men. The famous Three Brothers' Saloon occupies a position about midway the alley, and at its doors, the acme, the culminating point, the superlative degree of unquietude and discontent is reached. It is the headquarters of nearly all the great labor organizations in the city. Behind its doors, swinging as easily between the street and the liquor-fumed halls as the soul swings between right and wrong, the disturbed minds of the working-men become clouded, heated, and wrothily ready for deeds of violence.

Outside on the pavements with hundreds of like-excited men, with angry discussions and bitter recitals of complaints, the seeds of discord sown some time since, perhaps, sprout afresh, blossom and bear fruits. Is there a strike? Then special minions of the law are detailed to this place, for violence and hatred of employers, insurrection and socialism find here ready followers. Impromptu mass meetings are common, and law-breaking schemes find their cradle beneath its glittering lights. It is always thronged within and without, a veritable nursery of riot and disorder.

And oh, Bohemia, pipes, indolence and beer! The atmosphere is impregnated with it, the dust sifts it into your clothes and hair, the sunlight filters it through your brain, the stray snatches of music now and then beat it rhythmically into your mind. There are some who work, yes, and a few places outside of the saloons that seem to be animated with a business motive. There are even some who push their way briskly through the aimless bodies of men,—but then there must be an occasional anomaly to break the monotony, if nothing more.

It is so unlike the ordinary world, this bit of Bohemia, that one feels a personal grievance when the marble entrance and great, green dome become positive, solid, architectural facts, standing in all the grim solemnity of the main entrance of the Hotel Royal on St. Louis Street, ending, with a sudden return to aristocracy, this stamping ground for anarchy.

IMPRESSIONS.

THOUGHT.

A swift, successive chain of things,
   That flash, kaleidoscope-like, now in, now out,
Now straight, now eddying in wild rings,
   No order, neither law, compels their moves,
   But endless, constant, always swiftly roves.

HOPE.

Wild seas of tossing, writhing waves,
A wreck half-sinking in the tortuous gloom;
One man clings desperately, while Boreas raves,
   And helps to blot the rays of moon and star,
   Then comes a sudden flash of light, which gleams on shores afar.

LOVE.

A bed of roses, pleasing to the eye,
Flowers of heaven, passionate and pure,
Upon this bed the youthful often lie,
   And pressing hard upon its sweet delight,
   The cruel thorns pierce soul and heart, and cause a woeful blight.

DEATH.

A traveller who has always heard
That on this journey he some day must go,
   Yet shudders now, when at the fatal word
   He starts upon the lonesome, dreary way.
   The past, a page of joy and woe,—the future, none can say.

FAITH.

Blind clinging to a stern, stone cross,
   Or it may be of frailer make;
Eyes shut, ears closed to earth's drear dross,
   Immovable, serene, the world away
   From thoughts—the mind uncaring for another day.

SALAMMBÔ
BY GUSTAVE FLAUBERT.

Like unto the barbaric splendor, the clashing of arms, the flashing of jewels, so is this book, full of brightness that dazzles, yet does not weary, of rich mosaic beauty of sensuous softness. Yet, with it all, there is a singular lack of elevation of thought and expression; everything tends to degrade, to drag the mind to a worse than earthly level. The crudity of the warriors, the minute description of the battles, the leper, Hann; even the sensual love-scene of Salammbô and Matho, and the rites of Taint and Moloch. Possibly this is due to the peculiar shortness and crispness of the sentences, and the painstaking attention to details. Nothing is left for the imagination to complete. The slightest turn of the hand, the smallest bit of tapestry and armor,—all, all is described until one's brain becomes weary with the scintillating flash of minutia. Such careful attention wearies and disappoints, and sometimes, instead of photographing the scenes indelibly upon the mental vision, there ensues only a confused mass of armor and soldiers, plains and horses.

But the description of action and movement are incomparable, resembling somewhat, in the rush and flow of words, the style of Victor Hugo; the breathless rush and fire, the restrained passion and fury of a master-hand.

Throughout the whole book this peculiarity is noticeable—there are no dissertations, no pauses for the author to express his opinions, no stoppages to reflect,—we are rushed onward with almost breathless haste, and many times are fain to pause and re-read a sentence, a paragraph, sometimes a whole page. Like the unceasing motion of a column of artillery in battle, like the roar and fury of the Carthaginian's elephant, so is the torrent of Flaubert's eloquence—majestic, grand, intense, with nobility, sensuous, but never sublime, never elevating, never delicate.

As an historian, Flaubert would have ranked high—at least in impartiality. Not once in the whole volume does he allow his prejudices, his opinions, his sentiments to crop out. We lose complete sight of the author in his work. With marvellous fidelity he explains the movements, the vices and the virtues of each party, and with Shakespearean tact, he conceals his identity, so that we are troubled with none of that Byronic vice of 'dipping one's pen into one's self.'

Still, for all the historian's impartiality, he is just a trifle incorrect, here and there—the ancients mention no aqueduct in or near Carthage. Hann was not crucified outside of Tunis. The incident of the Carthaginian women cutting off their tresses to furnish strings for bows and catapults is generally conceded to have occurred during the latter portion of the third Punic War. And still another difficulty presents itself—Salammbô was supposed to have been the only daughter of Hamilcar; according to Flaubert she dies unmarried, or rather on her wedding day, and yet historians tell us that after the death of the elder Barca, Hannibal was brought up and watched over by Hamilcar's son-in-law, Hasdrubal. Can it be possible that the crafty Numidian King, Nari Havas, is the intrepid, fearless and whole-souled Hasdrubal? Or is it only another deviation from the beaten track of history? In a historical novel, however, and one so evidently arranged for dramatic effects, such lapses from the truth only heighten the interest and kindle the imagination to a brighter flame.

The school of realism of which Zola, Tolstoi, De Maupassant, and others of that ilk are followers, claims its descent from the author of *Salammbô*. Perhaps their claim is well-founded, perhaps not; we are inclined to believe that it is, for every page in this novel is crowded with details, often disgusting, which are generally left out in ordinary works. The hideous deformity, the rottenness and repulsiveness of the leper Hann is brought out in such vivid detail that we sicken and fain would turn aside in disgust. But go where one will, the ghastly, quivering, wretched picture is always before us in all its filth and splendid misery. The reeking horrors of the battlefields, the disgusting details of the army imprisoned in the defile of the battle-axe, the grimness of the sacrifices to the blood-thirsty god, Moloch, the wretchedness of Hamilcar's slaves are presented with every ghastly detail, with every degrading trick of expression. Picture after picture of misery and foulness arises and pursues us as the grim witches pursued the hapless Tam O'Shanter, clutching us in ghastly arms, clinging to us with grim and ghoulish tenacity.

Viewing the character through the genteel crystal of nineteenth century civilization, they are all barbarous, unnatural, intensified; but considering the age in which they lived—the tendencies of that age, the gods they worshipped, the practices in which they indulged,—they are all true to life, perfect in the depiction of their natures. Spendius is a true Greek, crafty, lying, deceitful, ungrateful. Hamilcar needs no novelist to crystallize his character in words, he always remains the same Hamilcar of history, so it is with Hann; but to Flaubert alone are we indebted for the hideous realism of his external aspect. Matho is a dusky son of Libya,—fierce, passionate, resentful, unbridled in his speech and action, swept by the hot breath of furious love as his native sands are swept by the burning simoon. Salammbô, cold and strange delving deep in the mysticism of the Carthaginian gods, living apart from human passions in her intense love for the goddess, Tanit; Salammbô, in the earnest excess of her religious fervor, eagerly accepting the mission given her by the puzzled Saracharabim; Salammbô, twining the gloomy folds of the python about her perfumed limbs; Salammbô, resisting, then yielding to the fierce love of Matho; Salammbô, dying when her erstwhile lover expires; Salammbô, in all her many phases reminds us of some early Christian martyr or saint, though the sweet spirit of the Great Teacher is hidden in the punctual devotion to the mysterious rites of Tanit. She is an inexplicable mixture of the tropical exotic and the frigid snow-flower,—a rich and rare growth that attracts and repulses, that interests and absorbs, that we admire—without loving, detest—without hating.

LEGEND OF THE NEWSPAPER.

Poets sing and fables tell us,
Or old folk lore whispers low,
Of the origin of all things,
Of the spring from whence they came,
Kalevala, old and hoary,
Æneid, Iliad, Æsop, too,
All are filled with strange quaint legends,
All replete with ancient tales,—

How love came, and how old earth,
Freed from chaos, grew for us,
To a green and wondrous spheroid,
To a home for things alive;
How fierce fire and iron cold,
How the snow and how the frost,—
All these things the old rhymes ring,
All these things the old tales tell.

Yet they ne'er sang of the beginning,
Of that great unbreathing angel,
Of that soul without a haven,
Of that gracious Lady Bountiful,
Yet they ne'er told how it came here;
Ne'er said why we read it daily,
Nor did they even let us guess why
We were left to tell the tale.

Came one day into the wood-land,
Muckintosh, the great and mighty,
Muckintosh, the famous thinker,
He whose brain was all his weapons,
As against his rival's soarings,
High unto the vaulted heavens,
Low adown the swarded earth,
Rolled he round his gaze all steely,
And his voice like music prayed:
"Oh, Creator, wondrous Spirit,
Thou who hast for us descended
In the guise of knowledge mighty,
And our brains with truth o'er-flooded;
In the greatness of thy wisdom,
Knowest not our limitations?
Wondrous thoughts have we, thy servants,
Wondrous things we see each day,
Yet we cannot tell our brethren,
Yet we cannot let them know,
Of our doings and our happenings,
Should they parted be from us?
Help us, oh, Thou Wise Creator,
From the fulness of thy wisdom,
Show us how to spread our knowledge,
And disseminate our actions,
Such as we find worthy, truly."

Quick the answer came from heaven;
Muckintosh, the famous thinker,
Muckintosh, the great and mighty,
Felt a trembling, felt a quaking,
Saw the earth about him open,
Saw the iron from the mountains
Form a quaint and queer machine,
Saw the lead from out the lead mines

Roll into small lettered forms,
Saw the fibres from the flax-plant,
Spread into great sheets of paper,
Saw the ink galls from the green trees
Crushed upon the leaden forms;
Muckintosh, the famous thinker,
Muckintosh, the great and mighty,
Felt a trembling, felt a quaking,
Saw the earth about him open,
Saw the flame and sulphur smoking,
Came the printer's little devil,
Far from distant lands the printer,
Man of unions, man of cuss-words,
From the depths of sooty blackness;
Came the towel of the printer;
Many things that Muckintosh saw,—
Galleys, type, and leads and rules,
Presses, press-men, quoins and spaces,
Quads and caps and lower cases.

But to Muckintosh bewildered,
All this passed as in a dream,
Till within his nervous hand,
Hand with joy and fear a-quaking,
Muckintosh, the great and mighty,
Muckintosh, the famous thinker,
Held the first of our newspapers.

A CARNIVAL JANGLE.

There is a merry jangle of bells in the air, an all-pervading sense of jester's noise, and the flaunting vividness of royal colors; the streets swarm with humanity,—humanity in all shapes, manners, forms,—laughing, pushing, jostling, crowding, a mass of men and women and children, as varied and as assorted in their several individual peculiarities as ever a crowd that gathered in one locality since the days of Babel.

It is Carnival in New Orleans; a brilliant Tuesday in February, when the very air effervesces an ozone intensely exhilarating—of a nature half spring, half winter—to make one long to cut capers. The buildings are a blazing mass of royal purple and golden yellow, and national flags, bunting and decorations that laugh in the glint of the Midas sun. The streets a crush of jesters and maskers, Jim Crows and clowns, ballet girls and Mephistos, Indians and monkeys; of wild and sudden flashes of music, of glittering pageants and comic ones, of befeathered and belled horses. A madding dream of color and melody and fantasy gone wild in an effervescent bubble of beauty that shifts and changes and passes kaleidoscope-like before the bewildered eye.

A bevy of bright-eyed girls and boys of that uncertainty of age that hovers between childhood and maturity, were moving down Canal Street when there was a sudden jostle with another crowd meeting them. For a minute there was a deafening clamor of laughter, cracking of whips, which all maskers carry, jingle and clatter of carnival bells, and the masked and unmasked extricated themselves and moved from each other's paths. But in the confusion a tall Prince of Darkness had whispered to one of the girls in the unmasked crowd: "You'd better come with us, Flo, you're wasting time in that tame gang. Slip off, they'll never miss you; we'll get you a rig, and show you what life is."

And so it happened that when a half hour passed, and the bright-eyed bevy missed Flo and couldn't find her, wisely giving up the search at last, that she, the quietest and most bashful of the lot, was being initiated into the mysteries of "what life is."

Down Bourbon Street and on Toulouse and St. Peter Streets there are quaint little old-world places, where one may be disguised effectually for a tiny consideration. Thither guided by the shapely Mephisto, and guarded by the team of jockeys and ballet girls, tripped Flo. Into one of the lowest-ceiled, dingiest and most ancient-looking of these disguise shops they stopped.

"A disguise for this demoiselle," announced Mephisto to the woman who met them. She was small and wizened and old, with yellow, flabby jaws and neck like the throat of an alligator, and straight, white hair that stood from her head uncannily stiff.

"But the demoiselle wishes to appear a boy, *un petit garcon?*" she inquired, gazing eagerly at Flo's long, slender frame. Her voice was old and thin, like the high quavering of an imperfect tuning fork, and her eyes were sharp as talons in their grasping glance.

"Mademoiselle does not wish such a costume," gruffly responded Mephisto.

"*Ma foi*, there is no other," said the ancient, shrugging her shoulders. "But one is left now, mademoiselle would make a fine troubadour."

"Flo," said Mephisto, "it's a dare-devil scheme, try it; no one will ever know it but us, and we'll die before we tell. Besides, we must; it's late, and you couldn't find your crowd."

And that was why you might have seen a Mephisto and a slender troubadour of lovely form, with mandolin flung across his shoulder, followed by a bevy of jockeys and ballet girls, laughing and singing as they swept down Rampart Street.

When the flash and glare and brilliancy of Canal Street have palled upon the tired eye, and it is yet too soon to go home, and to such a prosaic thing as dinner, and one still wishes for novelty, then it is wise to go in the lower districts. Fantasy and fancy and grotesqueness in the costuming and behavior of the maskers run wild. Such dances and whoops and leaps as these hideous Indians and devils do indulge in; such wild curvetings and great walks. And in the open squares, where whole groups do congregate, it is wonderfully amusing. Then, too, there is a ball in every available hall, a delirious ball, where one may dance all day for ten cents; dance and grow mad for joy, and never know who were your companions, and be yourself unknown. And in the exhilaration of the day, one walks miles and miles, and dances and curvets, and the fatigue is never felt.

In Washington Square, away down where Royal Street empties its stream of children and men into the broad channel of Elysian fields Avenue, there was a perfect Indian dance. With a little imagination one might have willed away the vision of the surrounding houses and fancied one's self again in the forest, where the natives were holding a sacred riot. The square was filled with spectators, masked and unmasked. It was amusing to watch these mimic Redmen, they seemed so fierce and earnest.

Suddenly one chief touched another on the elbow. "See that Mephisto and troubadour over there?" he whispered huskily.

"Yes, who are they?"

"I don't know the devil," responded the other quietly, "but I'd know that other form anywhere. It's Leon, see? I know those white hands like a woman's and that restless head. Ha!"

"But there may be a mistake."

"No. I'd know that one anywhere; I feel it's him. I'll pay him now. Ah, sweetheart, you've waited long, but you shall feast now!" He was caressing something long, and lithe, and glittering beneath his blanket.

In a masked dance it is easy to give a death-blow between the shoulders. Two crowds meet and laugh and shout and mingle almost inextricably, and if a shriek of pain should arise, it is not noticed in the din, and when they part, if one should stagger and fall bleeding to the ground, who can tell who has given the blow? There is naught but an unknown stiletto on the ground, the crowd has dispersed, and masks tell no tales anyway. There is murder, but by whom? for what? *Quien sabe?*

And that is how it happened on Carnival night, in the last mad moments of Rex's reign, a broken-hearted woman sat gazing wide-eyed and mute at a horrible something that lay across the bed. Outside the long sweet march music of many bands floated in in mockery, and the flash of rockets and Bengal lights illumined the dead, white face of the girl troubadour.

PAUL TO VIRGINIA.
FIN DE SIECLE.

I really must confess, my dear,
   I cannot help but love you,
For of all girls I ever knew,
   There's none I place above you;
But then you know it's rather hard,
   To dangle aimless at your skirt,
And watch your every movement so,
   For I am jealous, and you're a flirt.

There's half a score of fellows round,
   You smile at every one,
And as I think to pride myself for basking in the sun
Of your sweet smiles, you laugh at me,
   And treat me like a lump of dirt,
Until I wish that I were dead,
   For I am jealous, and you're a flirt.

I'm sorry that I've ever known
    Your loveliness entrancing,
Or ever saw your laughing eyes,
    With girlish mischief dancing;
'Tis agony supreme and rare
To see your slender waist a-girt
With other fellows' arms, you see,
    For I am jealous, and you're a flirt.

Now, girlie, if you'll promise me,
    To never, never treat me mean,
I'll show you in a little while,
    The best sweetheart you've ever seen;
You do not seem to know or care,
    How often you've my feelings hurt,
While flying round with other boys,
    For I am jealous, and you're a flirt.

THE MAIDEN'S DREAM.

The maid had been reading love-poetry, where the world lay bathed in moon-light, fragrant with dew-wet roses and jasmine, harmonious with the clear tinkle of mandolin and guitar. Then a lethargy, like unto that which steeps the senses, and benumbs the faculties of the lotus-eaters, enveloped her brain, and she lay as one in a trance,—awake, yet sleeping; conscious, yet unburdened with care.

And there stole into her consciousness, words, thoughts, not of her own, yet she read them not, nor heard them spoken; they fell deep into her heart and soul, softer and more caressing than the over-shadowing wing of a mother-dove, sweeter and more thrilling than the last high notes of a violin, and they were these:—

Love, most potent, most tyrannical, and most gentle of the passions which sway the human mind, thou art the invisible agency which rules mens' souls, which governs mens' kingdoms, which controls the universe. By thy mighty will do the silent, eternal hosts of Heaven sweep in sublime procession across the unmeasured blue. The perfect harmony of the spheres is attuned for thee, and by thee; the perfect coloring of the clouds, than which no mortal pigment can dare equal, are thy handiwork. Most ancient of the heathen deities, Eros; powerful God of the Christians, Jehovah, all hail! For a brief possession of thy divine fire have kingdoms waxed and waned; men in all the bitterness of hatred fought, bled, died by millions, their grosser selves to be swept into the bosom of their ancient mother, an immense holocaust to thee. For thee and thee alone does the world prosper, for thee do men strive to become better than their fellow-men; for thee, and through thee have they sunk to such depths of degradation as causes a blush to be painted upon the faces of those that see. All things are subservient to thee. All the delicate intricate workings of that marvellous machine, the human brain; all the passions and desires of the human heart,—ambition, desire, greed, hatred, envy, jealousy, all others. Thou breedst them all, O love, thou art all-potent, all-wise, infinite, eternal! Thy power is felt by mortals in all ages, all climes, all conditions. Behold!

A picture came into the maiden's eye: a broad and fertile plain, tender verdure, soft blue sky overhead, with white billowy clouds nearing the horizon like great airy, snow-capped mountains. The soft warm breeze from the south whispered faintly through the tall, slender palms and sent a thrill of joy through the frisky lambkins, who capered by the sides of their graver dams. And there among the riches of the flock stood Laban, haughty, stern, yet withal a kindly gleam in the glance which rested upon the group about him. Hoary the beard that rested upon his breast, but steady the hand that stretched in blessing. Leah, the tender-eyed, the slighted, is there; and Rachel, young and beautiful and blushing beneath the ardent gaze of her handsome lover. "And Jacob loved Rachel, and said, I will serve thee seven years for Rachel, thy younger daughter."

How different the next scene! Heaven's wrath burst loose upon a single community. fire, the red-winged demon with brazen throat wide opened, hangs his brooding wings upon an erstwhile happy city. Hades has climbed through the crater of Vesuvius, and leaps in fiendish waves along the land. Few the souls escaping, and God have mercy upon those who stumble through the blinding darkness, made more torturingly hideous by the intermittent flashes of lurid light. And yet there come three, whom the darkness seems not to deter, nor obstacles impede. Only a blind person, accustomed to constant darkness, and familiarized with these streets could walk that way. Nearer they come, a burst of flames thrown into the inky firmament by impish hands, reveals Glaucus, supporting the half-fainting Ione, following Nydia, frail, blind, flower-loving Nydia, sacrificing life for her unloving beloved.

And then the burning southern sun shone bright and golden o'er the silken sails of the Nile serpent's ships; glinted on the armor and weapons of the famous galley; shone with a warm caressing touch upon her beauty, as though it loved this queen, as powerful in her sphere as he in his. It is at Actium, and the fate of nations and generations yet unborn hang, as the sword of Damocles hung, upon the tiny thread of destiny. Egypt herself, her splendid barbaric beauty acting like an inspiration upon the craven followers, leads on, foremost in this fierce struggle. Then, the tide turns, and overpowered, they fly before disgrace and defeat. Antony is there, the traitor, dishonored, false to his country, yet true to his love; Antony, whom ambition could not lure from her passionate caresses; Antony, murmuring softly,—

> Egypt, thou knowest too well
> My heart was to thy rudder tied by the strings,
> And thou should'st tow me after.
> Over my spirit
> Thy full supremacy thou knewest,
> And that thy beck might from the bidding of the gods
> Command me.

Picture after picture flashed through the maiden's mind. Agnes, the gentle, sacrificing, burrowing like some frantic animal through the ruins of Lisbon, saving her lover, Franklin, by teeth and bleeding hands. Dora, the patient, serving a loveless existence, saving her rival from starvation and destitution. The stern, dark, exiled Florentine poet, with that one silver ray in his clouded life—Beatrice.

She heard the piping of an elfish voice, "Mother, why does the minister keep his hands over his heart?" and the white drawn face of Hester Prynne, with her scarlet elf-child, passed slowly across her vision. The wretched misery of deluded Lucius and his mysterious Lamia she saw, and watched with breathless interest the formation of that "Brotherhood of the Rose." There was radiant Armorel, from sea-blown, wave-washed Lyonesse, her perfect head poised in loving caress over the magic violin. Dark-eyed Corinne, head drooped gently as she improvised those Rome-famed world symphonies passed, almost ere Edna and St. Elmo had crossed the threshold of the church happy in the love now consecrated through her to God. Oh, the pictures, the forms, the love-words which crowded her mind! They thrilled her heart, crushed out all else save a crushing, over-powering sense of perfect, complete joy. A joy that sought to express itself in wondrous melodies and silences, filled with thoughts too deep and sacred for words. Overpowered with the magnificence of his reign, overwhelmed with the complete subjugation of all things unto him, do you wonder that she awoke and placing both hands into those of the lover at her side, whispered:—

>Take all of me—I am thine own, heart, soul,
>   Brain, body, all; all that I am or dream
>Is thine forever; yea, though space should teem
>With thy conditions, I'd fulfil the whole,
>Were to fulfil them to be loved by thee.

IN MEMORIAM.

The light streams through the windows arched high,
    And o'er the stern, stone carvings breaks
    In warm rich gold and crimson waves,
Then steals away in corners dark to die.

And all the grand cathedral silence falls
    Into the hearts of those that worship low,
    Like tender waves of hushed nothingness,
Confined nor kept by human earthly walls.

Deep music in its thundering organ sounds,
    Grows diffuse through the echoing space,
    Till hearts grow still in sadness' mighty joy,
Or leap aloft in swift ecstatic bounds.

Mayhap 'twas but a dream that came to me,
    Or but a vision of the soul's desire,
    To see the nation in one mighty whole,
Do homage on its bended, worshipping knee.

Through time's heroic actions, the soul of man,
    Alone proves what that soul without earth's dross
    Could be, and this, through time's far-searching fire,
Hath proved thine white beneath the deepest scan.

A woman's tribute, 'tis a tiny dot,
  A merest flower from a frail, small hand,
  To lay among the many petaled wreaths
About thy form,—a tribute soon forgot.

But if in all the incense to arise
  In fragrance to the blue empyrean
  The blended sweetness of the womens' love
Goes pouring too, in all their heartfelt sighs.

And if one woman's sorrow be among them too,
  One woman's joy for labor past
  Be reckoned in the mighty teeming whole,
It is enough, there is not more to do.

Within the hearts of heroes small and great
  There 'bides a tenderness for weakling things
  Within thy heart, the sorrowing country knows
These passions, bravest and the tenderest mate.

When man is dust, before the gazing eyes
  Of all the gaping throng, his life lies wide
  For all to see and whisper low about
Or let their thoughts in discord's clatter rise.

But thine was pure and undefiled,
  A record of long brilliant, teeming days,
  Each thought did tend to further things,
But pure as the proverbial child.

Oh, people, that thy grief might find express
  To gather in some vast cathedral's hall,
  That then in unity we might kneel and hear
Sublimity in sounds, voice our distress.

Peace, peace, the men of God cry, ye be bold,
   The world hath known, 'tis Heaven who claims him now,
   And in our railings we but cast aside
The noble traits he bid us hold.

So though divided through the land, in dreams
   We see a people kneeling low,
   Bowed down in heart and soul to see
This fearful sorrow, crushing as it seems.

And all the grand cathedral silence falls
   Into the hearts of these that worship low,
   Like tender waves of hushed nothingness,
Confined, nor kept by human earthly walls.

A STORY OF VENGEANCE.

Yes, Eleanor, I have grown grayer. I am younger than you, you know, but then, what have you to age you? A kind husband, lovely children, while I—I am nothing but a lonely woman. Time goes slowly, slowly for me now.

Why did I never marry? Move that screen a little to one side, please; my eyes can scarcely bear a strong light. Bernard? Oh, that's a long story. I'll tell you if you wish; it might pass an hour.

Do you ever think to go over the old school-days? We thought such foolish things then, didn't we? There wasn't one of us but imagined we would have only to knock ever so faintly on the portals of fame and they would fly wide for our entrance into the magic realms. On Commencement night we whispered merrily among ourselves on the stage to see our favorite planet, Venus, of course, smiling at us through a high, open window, "bidding adieu to her astronomy class," we said.

Then you went away to plunge into the most brilliant whirl of society, and I stayed in the beautiful old city to work.

Bernard was very much *en evidence* those days. He liked you a great deal, because in school-girl parlance you were my "chum." You say,—thanks, no tea, it reminds me that I'm an old maid; you say you know what happiness means—maybe, but I don't think any living soul could experience the joy I felt in those days; it was absolutely painful at times.

Byron and his counterparts are ever dear to the womanly heart, whether young or old. Such a man was he, gloomy, misanthropical, tired of the world, with a few dozen broken love-affairs among his varied experiences. Of course, I worshipped him secretly, what romantic, silly girl of my age, would not, being thrown in such constant contact with him.

One day he folded me tightly in his arms, and said:

"Little girl, I have nothing to give you in exchange for that priceless love of yours but a heart that has already been at another's feet, and a wrecked life, but may I ask for it?"

"It is already yours," I answered. I'll draw the veil over the scene which followed; you know, you've "been there."

Then began some of the happiest hours that ever the jolly old sun beamed upon, or the love-sick moon clothed in her rays of silver. Deceived me? No, no. He admitted that the old love for Blanche was still in his heart, but that he had lost all faith and respect for her, and could nevermore be other than a friend. Well, I was fool enough to be content with such crumbs.

We had five months of happiness. I tamed down beautifully in that time,—even consented to adopt the peerless Blanche as a model. I gave up all my most ambitious plans and cherished schemes, because he disliked women whose names were constantly in the mouth of the public. In fact, I became quiet, sedate, dignified, renounced too some of my best and dearest friends. I lived, breathed, thought, acted only for him; for me there was but one soul in the universe—Bernard's. Still, for all the suffering I've experienced, I'd be willing to go through it all again just to go over those five months. Every day together, at nights on the lake-shore listening to the soft lap of the waters as the silver sheen of the moon spread over the dainty curled waves; sometimes in a hammock swinging among the trees talking of love and reading poetry. Talk about Heaven! I just think there can't be a better time among the angels.

But there is an end to all things. A violent illness, and his father relenting, sent for the wayward son. I will always believe he loved me, but he was eager to get home to his mother, and anxious to view Blanche in the light of their new relationship. We had a whole series of parting scenes,—tears and vows and kisses exchanged. We clung to each other after the regulation fashion, and swore never to forget, and to write every day. Then there was a final wrench. I went back to my old life—he, away home.

For a while I was content, there were daily letters from him to read; his constant admonitions to practice; his many little tokens to adore—until there came a change,—letters less frequent, more mention of Blanche and her love for him, less of his love for me, until the truth was forced upon me. Then I grew cold and proud, and with an iron will crushed and stamped all love for him out of my tortured heart and cried for vengeance.

Yes, quite melo-dramatic, wasn't it? It is a dramatic tale, though.

So I threw off my habits of seclusion and mingled again with men and women, and took up all my long-forgotten plans. It's no use telling you how I succeeded. It was really wonderful, wasn't it? It seems as though that fickle goddess, Fortune, showered every blessing, save one, on my path. Success followed success, triumph succeeded triumph. I was lionized, feted, petted, caressed by the social and literary world. You often used to wonder how I stood it in all those years. God knows; with the heart-sick weariness and the fierce loathing that possessed me, I don't know myself.

But, mind you, Eleanor, I schemed well. I had everything seemingly that humanity craved for, but I suffered, and by all the gods, I swore that he should suffer too. Blanche turned against him and married his brother. An unfortunate chain of circumstances drove him from his father's home branded as a forger. Strange, wasn't it? But money is a strong weapon, and its long arm reaches over leagues and leagues of land and water.

One day he found me in a distant city, and begged for my love again, and for mercy and pity. Blanche was only a mistake, he said, and he loved me alone, and so on. I remembered all his thrilling tones and tender glances, but they might have moved granite now sooner than me. He knelt at my feet and pleaded like a criminal suing for life. I laughed at him and sneered at his misery, and told him what he had done for my happiness, and what I in turn had done for his.

Eleanor, to my dying day, I shall never forget his face as he rose from his knees, and with one awful, indescribable look of hate, anguish and scorn, walked from the room. As he neared the door, all the old love rose in me like a flood, drowning the sorrows of past years, and overwhelming me in a deluge of pity. Strive as I did, I could not repress it; a woman's love is too mighty to be put down with little reasonings. I called to him in terror, "Bernard, Bernard!" He did not turn; gave no sign of having heard.

"Bernard, come back; I didn't mean it!"

He passed slowly away with bent head, out of the house and out of my life. I've never seen him since, never heard of him. Somewhere, perhaps on God's earth he wanders outcast, forsaken, loveless. I have my vengeance, but it is like Dead Sea fruit, all bitter ashes to the taste. I am a miserable, heart-weary wreck,—a woman with fame, without love.

"Vengeance is an arrow that often falleth and smiteth the hand of him that sent it."

AT BAY ST. LOUIS.

Soft breezes blow and swiftly show
    Through fragrant orange branches parted,
A maiden fair, with sun-flecked hair,
    Caressed by arrows, golden darted.
The vine-clad tree holds forth to me
    A promise sweet of purple blooms,
And chirping bird, scarce seen but heard
    Sings dreamily, and sweetly croons
        At Bay St. Louis.

The hammock swinging, idly singing,
    Lissome nut-brown maid
    Swings gaily, freely, to-and-fro;
The curling, green-white waters casting cool, clear shade,
    Rock small, shell boats that go
In circles wide, or tug at anchor's chain,
As though to skim the sea with cargo vain,
        At Bay St. Louis.

    The maid swings slower, slower to-and-fro,
And sunbeams kiss gray, dreamy half-closed eyes;
    Fond lover creeping on with foot steps slow,
Gives gentle kiss, and smiles at sweet surprise.

    The lengthening shadows tell that eve is nigh,
    And fragrant zephyrs cool and calmer grow,
Yet still the lover lingers, and scarce breathed sigh,
    Bids the swift hours to pause, nor go,
        At Bay St. Louis.

NEW YEAR'S DAY.

The poor old year died hard; for all the earth lay cold
    And bare beneath the wintry sky;
While grey clouds scurried madly to the west,
    And hid the chill young moon from mortal sight.
Deep, dying groans the aged year breathed forth,
    In soughing winds that wailed a requiem sad
In dull crescendo through the mournful air.

The new year now is welcomed noisily
    With din and song and shout and clanging bell,
And all the glare and blare of fiery fun.
Sing high the welcome to the New Year's morn!
    Le roi est mort. Vive, vive le roi! cry out,
And hail the new-born king of coming days.

Alas! the day is spent and eve draws nigh;
The king's first subject dies—for naught,
And wasted moments by the hundred score
    Of past years rise like spectres grim
To warn, that these days may not idly glide away.
Oh, New Year, youth of promise fair!
    What dost thou hold for me? An aching heart?
Or eyes burnt blind by unshed tears? Or stabs,
    More keen because unseen?
Nay, nay, dear youth, I've had surfeit
    Of sorrow's feast. The monarch dead
Did rule me with an iron hand. Be thou a friend,
    A tender, loving king—and let me know
The ripe, full sweetness of a happy year.

THE UNKNOWN LIFE OF JESUS CHRIST.

A new gem has been added to sacred literature, and this is the accidental discovery by Nicolas Notovich of a Buddhist history of a phase of Christ's life left blank in the Scriptures.

Notovich, an adventurer, searching amid the ruins of India, delving deep in all the ancient Buddhistic lore, accidentally stumbles upon the name of Saint Issa, a renowned preacher, ante-dating some 2,000 years. The name becomes a wondrous attraction to Notovich, particularly as he learns through many Buddhist priests, Issa's name in juxtaposition with the Christian faith, and later, has reason to believe that the Jesus Christ of our religion and the Saint Issa of their tradition are identical.

Through a seemingly unfortunate accident, Notovich sustains an injury to his leg, and is cared for most tenderly by the monks of the convent of Himis. Despite his severe agonies, he retains consciousness and curiosity enough to plead for a glimpse of the wonderful documents contained in the archives of the convent, treating of the life of Saint Issa and the genealogy of the House of David. This he has translated and gives to the public.

Just whether to take the history seriously or not is a subject that requires much thought; but whether it be truth or fiction, whether the result of patient investigation and careful study of an interested scholar, or the wild imaginings of a feeble brain, it opens a wild field of speculation to the thoughtful mind.

The first three chapters of this history, contain a brief epitome of the Pentatouch of Moses. Though contrary to the teachings of tradition, Moses is said not to have written these books himself, but that they were transcribed generations after his time. According to this theory, then, the seeming imperfections and inconsistencies and tautological errors of the Old Testament as compared with the brief, clear, concise, logical statement of the Buddhists may readily be explained by the frailty of human memory, and the vividness of Oriental imagination.

Prince Mossa of the Buddhists, otherwise Moses of the Jews, was not, as is popularly supposed, a foundling of the Jews, or a protege of the Egyptian princess, but a full fledged prince, son of Pharaoh the mighty. This abrupt over-throw of the tradition of ages is like all disillusions, distasteful, but even the most superficial study of Egyptian customs and laws of that time will serve to impress us with the verity of this opinion. The law of caste was most rigidly and cruelly adhered to, and though all the pleadings and threatenings and weepings of the starry-eyed favorite of the harem may have been brought to bear upon this descendant of Rameses, yet is it probable that a descendant of an outcast race should receive the care and learning and advantages of a legally born prince? Hardly.

The condition of the ancient Israelites in the Christian Scriptures and in the Buddhist parchment are the same, yet there is reason to believe that the former was transcribed many centuries after the hieroglyphics of the latter became faded with age, hence, perhaps, the difference in the parentage of Moses.

"And Mossa was beloved throughout the land of Egypt for the goodness and compassion he displayed for them that suffered, pleaded with his father to soften the lot of these unhappy people, but Pharaoh became angry with him, and only imposed more hardships upon his slaves."

At this period in our Scriptures, the Lord communicates with Moses, and inflicts the plagues upon the nation, while in the manuscript of the Himis monks, the annual plague brought on by natural causes falls upon Egypt, and decimates the community. Here is a strange reversal of the order of things. In India, for ages the home of superstition and idol worship, that which has always been regarded by the Christians, the sworn enemies of the supernatural, as an inexplicable mystery, is accounted for by perfectly natural causes.

From that time, the fourth chapter of the chronicle of St. Issa corresponds exactly in its condensed form to the most prominent chronology of the Old Testament. With the beginning of the next chapter, the Divine Infant, through whom the salvation of the world was to come, appears upon the scene, as the first born of a poor but highly connected family, referring, presumably, to the ancestry of Joseph and Mary.

The remarkable wisdom of the child in earlier years is chronicled in our ancient parchment with as much care as in the vellum-bound volume of our church scriptures. At the age of twelve, the last glimpse we have of Jesus in the New Testament, is as a precocious boy, seated in the Temple, expounding the Scriptures to the learned members of the Sanhedrin. After that, we have no further sight of him, until sixteen years later, he re-appears at the marriage in Cana, a grown and serious man, already with well-formulated plans for the furtherance of his father's kingdom. This broad lapse in the Scriptures is filled by one simple sentence in the gospel of St. Luke. "And he was in the desert till the day of his showing into Israel." Where he was, why he had gone, and what he was doing are left to the imagination of the scholar and commentator.

Many theories have been advanced, and the one most accepted, was that he had followed the trade of his terrestrial father, Joseph, and was near Jerusalem among the tools of carpentry, helping his parents to feed the hungry mouths of his brothers and sisters.

But there appears another plausible theory advanced by the Buddhist historians, and sustained by the Buddhist traditions, that as Moses had fled into the wilderness to spend forty years in fasting and preparation for his life work, so Jesus had fled, not to the wilderness, but to the ancient culture and learning and the wisdom of centuries to prepare himself, by a knowledge of all religions for the day of the redemption.

Among the Jews of that day, and even among the more conservative descendants of Abraham yet, there existed, and exists a law which accustoms the marrying of the sons, especially the oldest son, at the age of thirteen. It is supposed that Issa, resisting the thraldom and carnal temptation of the marital state, fled from the importunities of the wise men, who would fain unite their offspring with such a wise and serious youth.

"It was then that Issa clandestinely left his father's house, went out of Jerusalem, and in company with some merchants, travelled toward Sinai."

"That he might perfect himself in the divine word and study the laws of the Great Buddha."

For six years he kept all India stirred to its utmost depths as he afterward kept all Palestine stirred by the purity of his doctrines, and the direct simplicity of his teachings. The white priests of Bramah gave him all their law, teaching him the language and religion of the dwellers of the five rivers. In Juggernaut, Rajegrilia, Benares, and other holy cities he was beloved by all. For true, here, as elsewhere, to his theory of the universal brotherhood of man, not only did he move among the upper classes, but also with the wretched Vaisyas and Soudras, the lowest of low castes who even were forbidden to hear the Vedas read, save only on feast days. Just as among the Jews, he was tolerant, merciful and kindly disposed towards the Samaritans, the Magdalens, the Lazaruses as to the haughty rabbis.

His impress upon the home of Buddha and Brahma was manifested by the hitherto unknown theory of monotheism, established by him, but gradually permitted to fall into desuetude, and become confounded with the polytheistic hierarchy of the confusing religion. Just as the grand oneness and simplicity of the Christian religion has been permitted to deteriorate into many petty sects, each with its absurd limitations, and its particular little method of worshipping the Great Father.

The teachings of Issa in India bear close relation in the general trend of thought to the teachings of Jesus among the multitudes about Jerusalem. There is the same universal simplicity of man's brotherhood; the complete self-abnegation of the flesh to the mind; the charitable impulses of a kind heart, and the utter disregard of caste, whether of birth, or breeding, or riches.

Of miracles in India, Issa says, "The miracles of our God began when the universe was created, they occur each day, each instant; whosoever does not see them, is deprived of one of the most beautiful gifts of life."

At last, according to the chronicles of the Buddhists, Issa was recalled from his labors in India to the land of Israel, where the people oppressed as of old by the Pharaohs, and now by the mighty men from the country of the Ramones, otherwise the Romans.

Here Pilate appears in a new light. Heretofore he has always been a passive figure in the story of the crucifixion. Indeed he is entirely exonerated from all blame by some of our religious bibliographers and made to appear in a philanthropic light, but the priests of Egypt, undeceived by the treacherous memories and careless chronicling on the disciples of old, place Pilate before us as a thorough Roman, greedy, crafty, cruel, unscrupulous. According to them he places a spy upon the actions of Jesus in the beginning of his three years teachings, who follows him in all his journeys, and in the end betrays him to the Romans. This person can be no other than Judas, the betrayer. And here we are permitted to view his seemingly inexplicable actions in a new light, and from being Judas, a sorrowing misanthrope, the erstwhile friend of Christ, he becomes merely a common enemy, the tool of the Romans.

Then we have the trial and death of Issa, strongly similar to our accepted version, and the chronicle briefly ends with the statement of the subsequent work of the disciples. The story of the Buddhist was written very shortly after the Passion of the Cross; the New Testament was transcribed years after the chief actors were dust.

We are so steeped in tradition, and so conservative on any subject that touches our religious beliefs that it is somewhat difficult to reconcile ourselves to another addition to our Scriptures. But if we should look at the matter earnestly, and give deep thought to the relative positions, lives, and endings of these two noble men, Issa and Christ, we could scarcely doubt that they are one. Without trying, as does the author, to break down with one fell swoop, the entire structure of the Bible, we cannot but admit the probability of the new theory.

It may be claimed that the remarkable personality of Christ would have left more of an impress upon India than it did, and that Christianity there and in India would have been synchronous, but we must remember, that there among the idols of Bramah and Vishnu, the way was not prepared, the people unexpectant of a new prophet, unwarned of him and unheeded. There he seems to have had no close personal followers to take up the work just where he left it, and continue. The dwellers of India were more happy in their entirety and more comfortable than the Jews, hence there was no Deliverer to impress them forever with the gigantic sacrifice of human frame and Divine soul.

St. Issa, one of the most revered prophets of the Buddhists, Jesus Christ, the Man and God of all other men, the divine incarnation of the ideal, are they the same? Why not?

IN OUR NEIGHBORHOOD.

The Harts were going to give a party. Neither Mrs. Hart, nor the Misses Hart, nor the small and busy Harts who amused themselves and the neighborhood by continually falling in the gutter on special occasions, had mentioned this fact to anyone, but all the interested denizens of that particular square could tell by the unusual air of bustle and activity which pervaded the Hart domicile. Lillian, the æsthetic, who furnished theme for many spirited discussions, leaned airily out of the window; her auburn (red) tresses carefully done in curl papers. Martha, the practical, flourished the broom and duster with unwonted activity, which the small boys of the neighborhood, peering through the green shutters of the front door, duly reported to their mammas, busily engaged in holding down their respective door-steps by patiently sitting thereon.

Pretty soon, the junior Harts,—two in number—began to travel to and fro, soliciting the loan of a "few chairs," "some nice dishes," and such like things, indispensable to every decent, self-respecting party. But to all inquiries as to the use to which these articles were to be put, they only vouchsafed one reply, "Ma told us as we wasn't to tell, just ask for the things, that's all."

Mrs. Tuckley the dress-maker, brought her sewing out on the front-steps, and entered a vigorous protest to her next-door neighbor.

"Humph," she sniffed, "mighty funny they can't say what's up. Must be something in it. Couldn't get none o' *my* things, and not invite *me!*"

"Did she ask you for any?" absent-mindedly inquired Mrs. Luke, shielding her eyes from the sun.

"No-o—, but she'd better sense, she knows *me*—she ain't—mercy me, Stella! Just look at that child tumbling in the mud! You, Stella, come here, I say! Look at you now, there—and there—and there?"

The luckless Stella having been soundly cuffed, and sent whimpering in the back-yard, Mrs. Tuckley continued,

"Yes as I was saying, 'course, taint none o' my business, but I alwaysways did wonder how them Harts do keep up. Why, them girls dress just as fine as any lady on the Avenue and that there Lillian wears real diamond ear-rings. 'Pears mighty, mighty funny to me, and Lord the airs they do put on! Holdin' up their heads like nobody's good enough to speak to. I don't like to talk about people, you know, yourself, Mrs. Luke I never speak about anybody, but mark my word, girls that cut up capers like them Hartses' girls never come to any good."

Mrs. Luke heaved a deep sigh of appreciation at the wisdom of her neighbor, but before she could reply a re-inforcement in the person of little Mrs. Peters, apron over her head, hands shrivelled and soap-sudsy from washing, appeared.

"Did you ever see the like?" she asked in her usual, rapid breathless way. "Why, my Louis says they're putting canvass cloths on the floor, and taking down the bed in the back-room; and putting greenery and such like trash about. Some style about them, eh?"

Mrs. Tuckley tossed her head and sniffed contemptuously, Mrs. Luke began to rehearse a time worn tale, how once a carriage had driven up to the Hart house at nine o'clock at night, and a distinguished looking man alighted, went in, stayed about ten minutes and finally drove off with a great clatter. Heads that had shaken ominously over this story before began to shake again, and tongues that had wagged themselves tired with conjectures started now with some brand new ideas and theories. The children of the square, tired of fishing for minnows in the ditches, and making mud-pies in the street, clustered about their mother's skirts receiving occasional slaps, when their attempts at taking part in the conversation became too pronounced.

Meanwhile, in the Hart household, all was bustle and preparation. To and fro the members of the house flitted, arranging chairs, putting little touches here and there, washing saucers and glasses, chasing the Hart Juniors about, losing things and calling frantically for each other's assistance to find them. Mama Hart, big, plump and perspiring, puffed here and there like a large, rosy engine, giving impossible orders, and receiving sharp answers to foolish questions. Lillian, the æsthetic, practiced her most graceful poses before the large mirror in the parlor; Martha rushed about, changing the order of the furniture, and Papa Hart, just come in from work, paced the rooms disconsolately, asking for dinner.

"Dinner!" screamed Mama Hart, "Dinner, who's got time to fool with dinner this evening? Look in the sideboard and you'll see some bread and ham; eat that and shut up."

Eight o'clock finally arrived, and with it, the music and some straggling guests. When the first faint chee-chee of the violin floated out into the murky atmosphere, the smaller portion of the neighborhood went straightway into ecstasies. Boys and girls in all stages of deshabille clustered about the door-steps and gave vent to audible exclamations of approval or disapprobation concerning the state of affairs behind the green shutters. It was a warm night and the big round moon sailed serenely in a cloudless, blue sky. Mrs. Tuckley had put on a clean calico wrapper, and planted herself with the indomitable Stella on her steps, "to watch the purceedings."

The party was a grand success. Even the intensely critical small fry dancing on the pavement without to the scraping and fiddling of the string band, had to admit that. So far as they were concerned it was all right, but what shall we say of the guests within? They who glided easily over the canvassed floors, bowed, and scraped and simpered, "just like the big folks on the Avenue," who ate the ice-cream and cake, and drank the sweet, weak Catawba wine amid boisterous healths to Mr. and Mrs. Hart and the Misses Hart; who smirked and perspired and cracked ancient jokes and heart-rending puns during the intervals of the dances, who shall say that they did not enjoy themselves as thoroughly and as fully as those who frequented the wealthier entertainments up-town.

Lillian and Martha in gossamer gowns of pink and blue flitted to and fro attending to the wants of their guests. Mrs. Hart, gorgeous in a black satin affair, all folds and lace and drapery, made desperate efforts to appear cool and collected—and failed miserably. Papa Hart spent one half his time standing in front of the mantle, spreading out his coat-tails, and benignly smiling upon the young people, while the other half was devoted to initiating the male portion of the guests into the mysteries of "snake killing."

Everybody had said that he or she had had a splendid time, and finally, when the last kisses had been kissed, the last good-byes been said, the whole Hart family sat down in the now deserted and disordered rooms, and sighed with relief that the great event was over at last.

"Nice crowd, eh?" remarked Papa Hart. He was brimful of joy and second-class whiskey, so no one paid any attention to him.

"But did you see how shamefully Maude flirted with Willie Howard?" said Lillian. Martha tossed her head in disdain; Mr. Howard she had always considered her especial property, so Lillian's observation had a rather disturbing effect.

"I'm so warm and tired," cried Mama Hart, plaintively, "children how are we going to sleep to-night?"

Thereupon the whole family arose to devise ways and means for wooing the drowsy god. As for the Hart Juniors they had long since solved the problem by falling asleep with sticky hands and faces upon a pile of bed-clothing behind the kitchen door.

It was late in the next day before the house had begun to resume anything like its former appearance. The little Harts were kept busy all morning returning chairs and dishes, and distributing the remnants of the feast to the vicinity. The ice-cream had melted into a warm custard, and the cakes had a rather worse for wear appearance, but they were appreciated as much as though just from the confectioner. No one was forgotten, even Mrs. Tuckley, busily stitching on a muslin garment on the steps, and unctuously rolling the latest morsel of scandal under her tongue, was obliged to confess that "them Hartses wasn't such bad people after all, just a bit queer at times."

About two o'clock, just as Lillian was re-draping the tidies on the stiff, common plush chairs in the parlor, some one pulled the bell violently. The visitor, a rather good-looking young fellow, with a worried expression smiled somewhat sarcastically as he heard a sound of scuffling and running within the house.

Presently Mrs. Hart opened the door wiping her hand, red and smoking with dish-water, upon her apron. The worried expression deepened on the visitor's face as he addressed the woman with visible embarrassment.

"Er—I—I—suppose you are Mrs. Hart?" he inquired awkwardly.

"That's my name, sir," replied she with pretentious dignity.

"Er—your-er—may I come in madam?"

"Certainly," and she opened the door to admit him, and offered a chair.

"Your husband is an employee in the fisher Oil Mills, is he not?"

Mrs. Hart straightened herself with pride as she replied in the affirmative. She had always been proud of Mr. Hart's position as foreman of the big oil mills, and was never so happy as when he was expounding to some one in her presence, the difficulties and intricacies of machine-work.

"Well you see my dear Mrs. Hart," continued the visitor. "Now pray don't get excited—there has been an accident, and your husband—has—er—been hurt, you know."

But for a painful whitening in her usually rosy face, and a quick compression of her lips, the wife made no sign.

"What was the accident?" she queried, leaning her elbows on her knees.

"Well, you see, I don't understand machinery and the like, but there was something about a wheel out of gear, and a band bursted, or something, anyhow a big wheel flew to pieces, and as he was standing near, he was hit."

"Where?"

"Well—well, I may as well tell you the truth, madam; a large piece of the wheel struck him on the head—and—he was killed instantly."

She did not faint, nor make any outcry, nor tear her hair as he had partly expected, but sat still staring at him, with a sort of helpless, dumb horror shining out her eyes, then with a low moan, bowed her head on her knees and shuddered, just as Lillian came in, curious to know what the handsome stranger had to say to her mother.

The poor mutilated body came home at last, and was laid in a stiff, silver-decorated, black coffin in the middle of the sitting-room, which had been made to look as uncomfortable and unnatural as mirrors and furniture shrouded in sheets and mantel and tables divested of ornaments would permit.

There was a wake that night to the unconfined joy of the neighbors, who would rather a burial than a wedding. The friends of the family sat about the coffin, and through the house with long pulled faces. Mrs. Tuckley officiated in the kitchen, making coffee and dispensing cheese and crackers to those who were hungry. As the night wore on, and the first restraint disappeared, jokes were cracked, and quiet laughter indulged in, while the young folks congregated in the kitchen, were hilariously happy, until some member of the family would appear, when every face would sober down.

The older persons contented themselves with recounting the virtues of the deceased, and telling anecdotes wherein he figured largely. It was astonishing how many intimate friends of his had suddenly come to light. Every other man present had either attended school with him, or was a close companion until he died. Proverbs and tales and witty sayings were palmed off as having emanated from his lips. In fact, the dead man would have been surprised himself, had he suddenly come to life and discovered what an important, what a modern solomon he had become.

The long night dragged on, and the people departed in groups of twos and threes, until when the gray dawn crept slowly over the blackness of night shrouding the electric lights in mists of cloudy blue, and sending cold chills of dampness through the house, but a few of the great crowd remained.

The day seemed so gray in contrast to the softening influence of the night, the grief which could be hidden then, must now come forth and parade itself before all eyes. There was the funeral to prepare for; the dismal black dresses and bonnets with their long crape veils to don; there were the condolences of sorrowing friends to receive; the floral offerings to be looked at. The little Harts strutted about resplendent in stiff black cravats, and high crape bands about their hats. They were divided between two conflicting emotions—joy at belonging to a family so noteworthy and important, and sorrow at the death. As the time for the funeral approached, and Lillian began to indulge in a series of fainting fits, the latter feeling predominated.

"Well it was all over at last, the family had returned, and as on two nights previous, sat once more in the deserted and dismantled parlor. Mrs. Tuckley and Mrs. Luke, having rendered all assistance possible, had repaired to their respective front steps to keep count of the number of visitors who returned to condole with the family.

"A real nice funeral," remarked the dress-maker at last, "a nice funeral. Everybody took it so hard, and Lillian fainted real beautiful. She's a good girl that Lillian. Poor things, I wonder what they'll do now."

Stella, the irrepressible, was busily engaged balancing herself on one toe, *a la* ballet.

"Mebbe she's goin' to get married," she volunteered eagerly, " 'cos I saw that yeller-haired young man what comes there all the time, wif his arms around her waist, and a tellin' her not to grieve as he'd take care of her. I was a peepin' in the dinin'-room."

"How dare you peep at other folks, and pry into people's affairs? I can't imagine where you get your meddlesome ways from. There aint none in *my family*. Next time I catch you at it, I'll spank you good." Then, after a pause, "Well what else did he say?"

FAREWELL.

Farewell, sweetheart, and again farewell;
To day we part, and who can tell
   If we shall e'er again
Meet, and with clasped hands
Renew our vows of love, and forget
   The sad, dull pain.

Dear heart, 'tis bitter thus to lose thee
And think mayhap, you will forget me;
   And yet, I thrill
As I remember long and happy days
Fraught with sweet love and pleasant memories
   That linger still

You go to loved ones who will smile
And clasp you in their arms, and all the while
   I stay and moan
For you, my love, my heart and strive
To gather up life's dull, gray thread
   And walk alone.

Aye, with you love the red and gold
Goes from my life, and leaves it cold
   And dull and bare,
Why should I strive to live and learn
And smile and jest, and daily try
   You from my heart to tare?

Nay, sweetheart, rather would I lie
Me down, and sleep for aye; or fly
   To regions far
Where cruel Fate is not and lovers live
Nor feel the grim, cold hand of Destiny
   Their way to bar.

I murmur not, dear love, I only say
Again farewell. God bless the day
   On which we met,
And bless you too, my love, and be with you
In sorrow or in happiness, nor let you
   E'er me forget.

LITTLE MISS SOPHIE.

When Miss Sophie knew consciousness again, the long, faint, swelling notes of the organ were dying away in distant echoes through the great arches of the silent church, and she was alone, crouching in a little, forsaken, black heap at the altar of the Virgin. The twinkling tapers seemed to smile pityingly upon her, the beneficent smile of the white-robed Madonna seemed to whisper comfort. A long gust of chill air swept up the aisles, and Miss Sophie shivered, not from cold, but from nervousness.

But darkness was falling, and soon the lights would be lowered, and the great, massive doors would be closed, so gathering her thin little cape about her frail shoulders, Miss Sophie hurried out, and along the brilliant noisy streets home.

It was a wretched, lonely little room, where the cracks let the boisterous wind whistle through, and the smoky, grimy walls looked cheerless and unhomelike. A miserable little room in a miserable little cottage in one of the squalid streets of the Third District that nature and the city fathers seemed to have forgotten.

As bare and comfortless the room, so was Miss Sophie's lonely life. She rented these four walls from an unkempt little Creole woman, whose progeny seemed like the promised offspring of Abraham,—multitudinous. The flickering life in the pale little body she scarcely kept there by the unceasing toil of a pair of bony hands, stitching, stitching, ceaselessly, wearyingly on the bands and pockets of pants. It was her bread, this monotonous, unending work, and though while days and nights constant labor brought but the most meagre recompense, it was her only hope of life.

She sat before the little charcoal brazier and warmed her transparent, needle-pricked fingers, thinking meanwhile of the strange events of the day. She had been up town to carry the great, black bundle of pants and vests to the factory and receive her small pittance, and on the way home stopped in at the Jesuit Church to say her little prayer at the altar of the calm, white Virgin. There had been a wondrous burst of music from the great organ as she knelt there, an over-powering perfume of many flowers, the glittering dazzle of many lights, and the dainty frou-frou of silken skirts of wedding guests filing and tripping. So Miss Sophie stayed to the wedding, for what feminine heart, be it ever so old and seared, does not delight in one? And why shouldn't a poor little Creole old maid be interested too?

When the wedding party had filed in solemnly, to the rolling, swelling, pealing tones of the organ. Important-looking groomsmen, dainty, fluffy, white-robed maids, stately, satin-robed, illusion-veiled bride, and happy groom. She leaned forward to catch a better glimpse of their faces. Ah!—

Those near the Virgin's altar who heard a faint sigh and rustle on the steps glanced curiously as they saw a slight, black-robed figure clutch the railing and lean her head against it. Miss Sophie had fainted.

"I must have been hungry," she mused over the charcoal fire in her little room, "I must have been hungry," and she smiled a wan smile, and busied herself getting her evening meal of coffee and bread and ham.

If one were given to pity, the first thought that would rush to one's lips at sight of Miss Sophie would have been: Poor little Miss Sophie! She had come among the bareness and sordidness of this neighborhood five years ago, robed in crepe, and crying with great sobs that seemed to fairly shake the vitality out of her. Perfectly silent, too, about her former life, but for all that, Michel, the quarter grocer at the corner, and Mme. Laurent, who kept the rabbe shop opposite, had fixed it all up between them, of her sad history and past glories. Not that they knew, but then Michel must invent something when the neighbors came to him, their fountain head of wisdom.

One morning little Miss Sophie opened wide her dingy windows to catch the early freshness of the autumn wind as it whistled through the yellow-leafed trees. It was one of those calm, blue-misted, balmy, November days that New Orleans can have when all the rest of the country is fur-wrapped. Miss Sophie pulled her machine to the window, where the sweet, damp wind could whisk among her black locks.

Whirr, whirr, went the machine, ticking fast and lightly over the belts of the rough jean pants. Whirr, whirr, yes, and Miss Sophie was actually humming a tune! She felt strangely light to-day.

"*Ma foi,*" muttered Michel, strolling across the street to where Mme. Laurent sat sewing behind the counter on blue and brown-checked aprons, "but the little ma'amselle sings. Perhaps she recollects."

"Perhaps," muttered the rabbe woman.

But little Miss Sophie felt restless. A strange impulse seemed drawing her up town, and the machine seemed to run slow, slow, before it would stitch the endless number of jean belts. Her fingers trembled with nervous haste as she pinned up the unwieldy black bundle of the finished work, and her feet fairly tripped over each other in their eagerness to get to Claiborne Street, where she could board the up-town car. There was a feverish desire to go somewhere, a sense of elation,—foolish happiness that brought a faint echo of color into her pinched cheeks. She wondered why.

No one noticed her in the car. Passengers on the Claiborne line are too much accustomed to frail, little black-robed women with big, black bundles; it is one of the city's most pitiful sights. She leaned her head out of the window to catch a glimpse of the oleanders on Bayou Road, when her attention was caught by a conversation in the car.

"Yes, it's too bad for Neale, and lately married too," said the elder man, "I can't see what he is to do."

Neale! she pricked up her ears. That was the name of the groom in the Jesuit church.

"How did it happen?" languidly inquired the younger. He was a stranger, evidently; a stranger with a high regard for the faultlessness of male attire, too.

"Well, the firm failed first; he didn't mind that much, he was so sure of his uncle's inheritance repairing his lost fortunes, but suddenly this difficulty of identification springs up, and he is literally on the verge of ruin."

"Won't some of you fellows who've known him all your lives do to identify him?"

"Gracious man, we've tried, but the absurd old will expressly stipulates that he shall be known only by a certain quaint Roman ring, and unless he has it—no identification, no fortune. He has given the ring away and that settles it."

"Well, you're all chumps. Why doesn't he get the ring from the owner?"

"Easily said—but—It seems that Neale had some little Creole love-affair some years ago and gave this ring to his dusky-eyed fiancee. But you know how Neale is with his love-affairs, went off and forgot the girl in a month. It seems, however, she took it to heart,—so much so until he's ashamed to try to find her or the ring."

Miss Sophie heard no more as she gazed out into the dusty grass. There were tears in her eyes, hot blinding ones that wouldn't drop for pride, but stayed and scalded. She knew the story with all its embellishments of heartaches. The ring, too; she remembered the day she had kissed and wept and fondled it, until it seemed her heart must burst under its load of grief before she took it to the pawn broker's that another might be eased before the end came,—that other, her father. The "little Creole love affair" of Neale's had not always been poor and old and jaded-looking; but reverses must come, even Neale knew that—so the ring was at the *Mont de Piete*.

Still he must have it, it was his; it would save him from disgrace and suffering, and from trailing the proud head of the white-gowned bride into sorrow. He must have it,—but how?

There it was still at the pawn broker's, no one would have such a jewel, and the ticket was home in the bureau drawer. Well, he must have it; she might starve in the attempt. Such a thing as going to him and telling him that he might redeem it was an impossibility. That good, straight-backed, stiff-necked Creole blood would have risen in all its strength and choked her. No; as a present had the quaint Roman circlet been placed upon her finger,—as a present should it be returned.

The bumping car rode heavily, and the hot thoughts beat heavily in her poor little head. He must have the ring—but how—the ring—the Roman ring—the white-robed bride starving—she was going mad—ah yes,—the church.

Right in the busiest, most bustling part of the town, its fresco and bronze and iron quaintly suggestive of mediæval times. Within, all cool and dim and restful, with the faintest whiff of lingering incense rising and pervading the gray arches. Yes, the Virgin would know and have pity; the sweet, white-robed Virgin at the pretty flower-decked altar, or the one away up in the niche, far above the golden dome where the Host was. Holy Mary, Mother of God. Poor little Miss Sophie.

Titiche, the busy-body of the house, noticed that Miss Sophie's bundle was larger than usual that afternoon. "Ah, poor woman!" sighed Titiche's mother, "she would be rich for Christmas."

The bundle grew larger each day, and Miss Sophie grew smaller. The damp, cold rain and mist closed the white-curtained window, but always there behind the sewing machine drooped and bobbed the little black-robed figure. Whirr, whirr went the wheels, and the coarse jean pants piled in great heaps at her side. The Claiborne street car saw her oftener than before, and the sweet, white Virgin in the flowered niche above the gold-domed altar smiled at the little penitent almost every day.

"*Ma foi,*" said the slatternly landlady to Madame Laurent and Michel one day, "I no see how she live! Eat? Nothing, nothing, almost, and las' night when it was so cold and foggy, eh? I hav' to mek him build fire. She mos' freeze."

Whereupon the rumor spread that Miss Sophie was starving herself to death to get some luckless relative out of jail for Christmas, —a rumor which enveloped her scraggy little figure with a kind of halo to the neighbors when she appeared on the streets.

November had verged into December and the little pile of coins were yet far from the sum needed. Dear God! how the money did have to go. The rent, and the groceries and the coal,—though, to be sure, she used a precious bit of that. All the work and saving and skimping,—maybe, yes, maybe by Christmas. What a gift!

Christmas Eve night on Royal Street is no place for a weakling, for the shouts and carousals of the roisterers will strike fear into the brave. Yet amid the cries and yells, the deafening blow of horns and tin whistles and the really dangerous fusillade of fireworks, the little figure hurried along, one hand clutching tight the battered hat that the rude merry-makers would have torn off, the other grasping under the thin, black cape a worn little pocketbook.

Into the *Mont de Piete,* breathless, eager. The ticket? Here, worn, crumpled. The ring? It was not gone? No, thank Heaven! It was really a joy well worth her toil, she thought, to have it again.

Had Titiche not been shooting crackers on the banquette instead of peering into the crack, as was his wont, his big, round, black eyes would have grown saucer-wide to see little Miss Sophie kiss and fondle a ring, an ugly clumsy band of gold.

"Ah, dear ring," she murmured, "once you were his, and you shall be his again. You shall be on his finger, and perhaps touch his heart. Dear ring, *ma chere petite, de ma coeur, cheri, de ma coeur. Je t'aime, je t'aime, oui, oui.* You are his, you were mine once too. To-night, just one night, I'll keep you—then—tomorrow, where you can save him.

"Ah, the Virgin—she smiles at me because I did right, did I not sweet mother? She smiles—and—I grow—faint—"

The loud whistles and horns of the little ones rose on the balmy air next morning. No one would doubt it was Christmas Day, even if doors and windows are open wide to let in cool air.

Why, there was Christmas even in the very look of the mules on the poky cars; there was Christmas noise in the streets, and Christmas toys and Christmas odors, savory ones that made the nose wrinkle approvingly, issuing from the kitchen. Michel and Mme. Laurent smiled greetings across the street at each other, and the salutation from a passer-by recalled the many progenied landlady to herself.

"Miss Sophie, well, poor soul, not very much Christmas for her.

Mais, I'll just call her in to spend the day with me. It'll cheer her a bit."

So clean and orderly within the poor little room. Not a speck of dust or a litter of any kind on the quaint little old-time high bureau, unless you might except a sheet of paper lying loose with something written on it. Titiche had evidently inherited his prying propensities for the landlady turned it over and read:

"Louis. Here is the ring. I return it to you. I heard you needed it, I hope it comes not too late. Sophie."

"The ring, where?" muttered the landlady. There it was, clasped between her fingers on her bosom. A bosom, white and cold, under a cold, happy face. Christmas had indeed dawned for Miss Sophie —the eternal Christmas.

IF I HAD KNOWN.

If I had known
Two years ago how drear this life should be,
And crowd upon itself allstrangely sad,
Mayhap another song would burst from out my lips,
Overflowing with the happiness of future hopes;
Mayhap another throb than that of joy.
Have stirred my soul into its inmost depths,
      If I had known.

If I had known,
Two years ago the impotence of love,
The vainness of a kiss, how barren a caress,
Mayhap my soul to higher things have soarn,
Nor clung to earthly loves and tender dreams,
But ever up aloft into the blue empyrean,
And there to master all the world of mind,
      If I had known.

CHALMETLE.

Wreaths of lilies and immortelles,
Scattered upon each silent mound,
Voices in loving remembrance swell,
Chanting to heaven the solemn sound.
Glad skies above, and glad earth beneath;
And grateful hearts who silently
Gather earth's flowers, and tenderly wreath
Woman's sweet token of fragility.

Ah, the noble forms who fought so well
Lie, some unnamed, 'neath the grassy mound;
Heroes, brave heroes, the stories tell,
Silently too, the unmarked mounds,
Tenderly wreath them about with flowers,
Joyously pour out your praises loud;
For every joy beat in these hearts of ours
Is only a drawing us nearer to God.

Little enough is the song we sing,
Little enough is the tale we tell,
When we think of the voices who erst did ring
Ere their owners in smoke of battle fell.
Little enough are the flowers we cull
To scatter afar on the grass-grown graves,
When we think of bright eyes, now dimmed and dull
For the cause they loyally strove to save.

And they fought right well, did these brave men,
For their banner still floats unto the breeze,
And the pæans of ages forever shall tell
Their glorious tale beyond the seas.
Ring out your voices in praises loud,
Sing sweet your notes of music gay,
Tell me in all you loyal crowd
Throbs there a heart unmoved to-day?

Meeting together again this year,
As met we in fealty and love before;
Men, maids, and matrons to reverently hear
Praises of brave men who fought of yore.
Tell to the little ones with wondering eyes,
The tale of the flag that floats so free;
Till their tiny voices shall merrily rise
In hymns of rejoicing and praises to Thee.

Many a pure and noble heart
Lies under the sod, all covered with green;
Many a soul that had felt the smart
Of life's sad torture, or mayhap had seen
The faint hope of love pass afar from the sight,
Like swift flight of bird to a rarer clime
Many a youth whose death caused the blight
Of tender hearts in that long, sad time.

Nay, but this is no hour for sorrow;
They died at their duty, shall we repine?
Let us gaze hopefully on to the morrow
Praying that our lives thus shall shine.
Ring out your bugles, sound out your cheers!
Man has been God-like so may we be.
Give cheering thanks, there dry up those tears,
Widowed and orphaned, the country is free!

Wreathes of lillies and immortelles,
Scattered upon each silent mound,
Voices in loving remembrance swell,
Chanting to heaven the solemn sound,
Glad skies above, and glad earth beneath,
And grateful hearts who silently
Gather earth's flowers, and tenderly wreath
Woman's sweet token of fragility.

AT EVENTIDE.

All day had she watched and waited for his coming, and still her strained ears caught no sounds of the footsteps she loved and longed to hear. All day while the great sun panted on his way around the brazen skies; all day while the busy world throbbed its mighty engines of labor, nor witted of the breaking hearts in its midst. And now when the eve had come, and the sun sank slowly to rest, casting his red rays over the earth he loved, and bidding tired nature a gentle radiant good-night, she still watched and waited. Waited while the young moon shone silvery in the crimson flush of the eastern sky, while the one bright star trembled as he strove to near his love; waited while the hum of soul-wearing traffic died in the distant streets, and the merry voices of happy children floated to her ears.

And still he came not. What kept him from her side? Had he learned the cold lesson of self-control, or found one other thing more potent than love? Had some cruel chain of circumstances forced him to disobey her bidding—or—did he love another? But no, she smiles triumphantly, he could not having known and loved her.

Sitting in the deep imbrasure of the window through which the distant wave sounds of city life floated to her, the pages of her life seemed to turn back, and she read the almost forgotten tale of long ago, the story of their love. In those days his wish had been her law; his smile her sun; his frown her wretchedness. Within his arms, earth seemed a far-away dream of empty nothingness, and when his lips touched and clung to hers, sweet with the perfume of the South they floated away into a Paradise of enfolding space, where Time and Death and the woes of this great earth are naught, only these two—and love, the almighty.

And so their happiness drifted slowly across the sea of Time until it struck a cruel rock, whose sharp teeth showed not above the dimpled waves; and where once had been a craft of strength and beauty, now was only a hideous wreck. For the Tempter had come into this Eden, and soon his foul whisper found place in her heart.

And the Tempter's name was Ambition.

Often had the praises and plaudits of men rang in her ears when her sweet voice sang to her chosen friends, often had the tears evoked by her songs of love and hope and trust, thrilled her breast faintly, as the young bird stirs in its nest under the loving mother's wing, but he had clasped his arms around her, and that was enough. But one day the Tempter whispered, "Why waste such talent; bring that beauty of voice before the world and see men bow in homage, and women envy and praise. Come forth and follow me."

But she put him fiercely aside, and cried, "I want no homage but his, I want no envy from any one."

Still the whisper stayed in her heart, nor would the honeyed words of praise be gone, even when he kissed her, and thanked the gods for this pearl of great price.

Then as time fled on, the tiny whisper grew into a great roar, and all the praise of men, and the sweet words of women, filled her brain, and what had once been her aversion became a great desire, and caused her brow to grow thoughtful, and her eyes moody.

But when she spoke to him of this new love, he smiled and said, "My wife must be mine, and mine alone. I want not a woman whom the world claims, and shouts her name abroad. My wife and my home must be inviolate." And again as of yore, his wish controlled her—but only for a while.

Then the tiny whisper grown into the great roar urging her on, became a mighty wind which drove her before it, nor could she turn aside from the path of ambition, but swept on, and conquered.

Ah, sweet, sweet the exultation of the victor! Dear the plaudits of the admiring world; wild the joy, when queen of song, admired of men, she stood upon the pinnacle of fame! And he? True to his old convictions, turned sadly from the woman who placed the admiration of the world before his love and the happiness of his home—and went out from her life broken-hearted, disappointed, miserable.

All these things, and more, she thought upon in the first flush of eventide, as the bold, young star climbed toward his lady-love, the moon, all these things, and what had come to pass after the victory.

For there came a day when the world wearied of its toy, and turned with shouts of joy, and wreaths of fresh laurels for the new star. Then came disappointments and miseries crowding fast upon her; the sorrows which a loving heart knows when it finds its idols faithless. Then the love for him which she had once repressed arose in all its strength which had gained during the long struggle with the world, arose and overwhelmed her with its might, and filled her soul with an unutterable longing for peace and rest and him.

She wrote to him and told him all her heart, and begged of him to come back to her, for Fame was but an empty bubble while love was supreme and the only happiness, after all. And now she waited while the crimson and gold of the west grew dark, and gray and lowering.

Hark! She hears his loved step. He comes, ah, joy of heaven he comes! Soon will he clasp her in his arms, and there on his bosom shall she know peace and rest and love.

As he enters the door she hastens to meet him, the love-light shining in her tired eyes, her soft rounded arms outstretched to meet him. But he folds her not in his embrace, nor yet does he look with love into her upturned eyes; the voice she loves, ah so well, breaks upon the dusky silence, pitiless, stern.

"Most faithless of faithless women, think you that like the toy of a fickle child I can be thrown aside, then picked up again? Think you that I can take a soiled lily to my bosom? Think you that I can cherish the gaudy sun-flower that ever turns to the broad, brazen glare of the uncaring sun, rather than the modest shrinking violet? Nay, be not deceived, I loved you once, but that love you killed in its youth and beauty leaving me to stand and weep alone over its grave. I came to-night, not to kiss you, and to forgive you as you entreat, but to tell that you I have wed another."

The pitiless voice ceased, and she was alone in the dusky silence; alone in all the shame and agony and grief of unrequited love and worthless fame. Alone to writhe and groan in despair while the roseate flush of eventide passed into the coldness of midnight.

Oh faithless woman, oh, faithless man! How frail the memory of thy binding vows, thy blissful hours of love! Are they forgotten? Only the record of broken hearts and loveless lives will show.

THE IDLER.

An idle lingerer on the wayside's road,
He gathers up his work and yawns away;
A little longer, ere the tiresome load
Shall be reduced to ashes or to clay.

No matter if the world has marched along,
And scorned his slowness as it quickly passed;
No matter, if amid the busy throng,
He greets some face, infantile at the last.

His mission? Well, there is but one,
And if it is a mission he knows it, nay,
To be a happy idler, to lounge and sun,
And dreaming, pass his long-drawn days away.

So dreams he on, his happy life to pass
Content, without ambition's painful sighs,
Until the sands run down into the glass;
He smiles—content—unmoved and dies.

And yet, with all the pity that you feel
For this poor mothling of that flame, the world;
Are you the better for your desperate deal,
When you, like him, into infinitude are hurled?

LOVE AND THE BUTTERFLY.

I heard a merry voice one day
And glancing at my side,
Fair Love, all breathless, flushed with play,
A butterfly did ride.
"Whither away, oh sportive boy?"
I asked, he tossed his head;
Laughing aloud for purest joy,
And past me swiftly sped.

Next day I heard a plaintive cry
And Love crept in my arms;
Weeping he held the butterfly,
Devoid of all its charms.
Sweet words of comfort, whispered I
Into his dainty ears,
But Love still hugged the butterfly,
And bathed its wounds with tears.

THE BEE-MAN.

We were glancing over the mental photograph album, and commenting on the great lack of dissimilarity in tastes. Nearly every one preferred spring to any other season, with a very few exceptions in favor of autumn. The women loved Mrs. Browning and Longfellow; the men showed decided preferences after Emerson and Macauley. Conceit stuck out when the majority wanted to be themselves and none other, and only two did not want to live in the 19th century. But in one place, in answer to the question, "Whom would you rather be, if not yourself?" the answer was,

"A baby!"

"Why would you rather be a baby than any other personage?" queried someone glancing at the writer, who blushed as she replied.

"Because then I might be able to live a better life, I might have better opportunities and better chances for improving them, and it would bring me nearer the 20th century."

"About eight or nine years ago," said the first speaker, "I remember reading a story in a magazine for young folks. It was merely a fairy story, and perhaps was not intended to point a moral, but only to amuse the little ones. It was something on this order:—"

Once upon a time, there lived in an out of the way spot an ancient decrepit Bee-man. How old he was no one knew; whence he came, no one could tell: to the memory of the oldest inhabitant he had always lived in his dirty hut, surrounded by myriads of hives, attended always by a swarm of bees. He was good to the bits of children, and always ready with a sweet morsel of honeycomb for them. All his ambitions, sympathies and hopes were centered in his hives; until one day a fairy crept into his hut and whispered:

"You have not always been a common bee-man. Once you were something else."

"Tell me what I was," he asked eagerly.

"Nay, that I cannot do," replied the fairy, "our queen sent me to tell you this, and if you wished to search for your former self, I am to assist you. You must search the entire valley, and the first thing you meet to which you become violently attached, that is what you formerly were, and I shall give you back your correct form."

So the next morning the Bee-man, strapping his usual hive upon his back, and accompanied by the fairy in the form of a queen bee, set out upon his search throughout the valley. At first he became violently attached to the handsome person and fine castle of the Lord of the Realm, but on being kicked out of the lord's domains, his love turned to dislike.

The Bee-man and the fairy travelled far and wide and carefully inspected every thing they met. The very Imp, the Languid young man, the Hippogriffith, the Thousand Tailed Hippopotamus, and many other types, until the Bee-man grew weary and was about to give up the search in disgust.

But suddenly amid all the vast halls of the enchanted domains through which they were wandering, there sounded shrieks and wails, and the inmates were thrown into the greatest confusion by the sight of the hideous hippogriffith dashing through, a million sparks emanating from his great eyes, his barbed tail waving high in the air, and holding in his talons a tiny infant.

Now, as soon as the Bee-man saw this, a great wave of sorrow and pity filled his breast, and he hastily followed the monster, arriving at his cave just in time to see him preparing to devour his prey. Madly dashing his hive of bees into the hippogriffith's face, and seizing the infant while the disturbed and angry bees stung and swarmed, the Bee-man rushed out followed by the Very Imp, the Languid young man and the fairy, and made his way to the child's mother. Just as soon as the baby was safely restored, the Bee-man ruminated thoughtfully awhile and finally remarked to the fairy:

"Do you know of all the things I have met so far, I liked the baby best of all, so I think I must have been a baby once!"

"Right you are," assented the fairy, "I knew it before, but, of course, I couldn't tell. Now I shall change you into your former shape, but remember, you must try to be something better than a Bee-man."

The Bee-man promised and was instantly changed into a baby. The fairy inoculated him from harm with a bee-sting, and gave him to the rescued infant's mother.

Nearly a cycle passed by, and one day the fairy having business in the valley, thought she would make inquiries concerning her protege. In her way she happened to pass a little, low, curious hut, with many bee hives about it, and swarms of bees flying in and out. The fairy, tired as well as curious, peeped in and discovered an ancient man attending to the wants of his pets. Upon a closer inspection, she recognized her infant of years ago. He had become a bee-man again!

"It points a pretty little moral," said the Fatalist, "for it certainly proves that do what we will, we cannot get away from our natures. It was inherent in that man's nature to tend bees. Bee-ing was the occupation chosen for him by Fate, and had the beneficent Fairy changed him a dozen times, he would ultimately have gone to bee-ing in some form or other."

The Fatalist was doubtless right, for it seems as though the inherent things in our nature must come out. But if we want to dig deep into the child's story for metaphysical morals, does it not also uphold the theory of re-incarnation? The ancient bee-man, perhaps is but a type of humanity growing old, and settled in its mode of living, while the fairy is but thought, whispering into our souls things half dread half pleasant.

There are moments when the consciousness of a former life comes sharply upon us, in swift, lightning flashes, too sudden to be tangible, too dazzling to leave an impress, or mayhap, in troubled dreams that bewilder and confuse with vague remembrances. If only a burst of memory would come upon some mortal, that the tale might be fully told, and these theories established as facts. It would unfold great possibilities of historical lore; of literary life; of religious speculation.

AMID THE ROSES.

There is tropical warmth and languorous life
   Where the roses lie
   In a tempting drift
Of pink and red and golden light
Untouched as yet by the pruning knife.
And the still, warm life of the roses fair
   That whisper "Come,"
   With promises
Of sweet caresses, close and pure
Has a thorny whiff in the perfumed air.
There are thorns and love in the roses' bed,
   And Satan too
   Must linger there;
So Satan's wiles and the conscience stings,
Must now abide—the roses are *dead*.

Alice Ruth Moore Dunbar Nelson (1875–1935) was an American poet, journalist, and political activist. Among the first generation born free in the South after the Civil War, she was a prominent figure involved in the artistic flourishing of the Harlem Renaissance. A bisexual, multiracial Creole, she traveled across the country lecturing in support of African Americans' and women's rights.

Manufactured by Amazon.ca
Acheson, AB